I0598961

From Now On, You're Back

stories

Richard Weems

WbW Ink

New Jersey

For Svea, my BabyMine.

CONTENTS

ACKNOWLEDGMENTS

Thanks to the following publications for first publishing previous versions of these stories:

North American Review - "From Now On, You're Back,"
"John & Xenia: and "A Murder During the Reagan Era"
Local Knowledge - "The Easter Bunny Effect" and "First
Thanksgiving"
Dogwood - "A Memorial for Hammerhead"
The Del Sol Review - "Dangerous Lightning"
Alligator Juniper - "MasterBlaster"
Alkali Flats - "Real Grief"

FROM NOW ON, YOU'RE BACK

My brother Henry called at three a.m. to see if I would pull some strings for him at the bank where I worked. He was drunk and obsessed with buying a house. He wanted to settle down, straighten out. "I want to sail a tight ship," he said, "just like my little brother." I took the call down in the living room, but the damage was already done: Joan paced the upstairs hall while our son wriggled and screamed in her arms.

"I got references," Henry offered in his defense. I could almost smell his breath.

"I can't discuss this now," I said, but Henry kept on about how he was bound to make assistant manager at Denny's in a few months. He'd found the perfect house, the woman he wanted to wind out his life with, though he wouldn't tell me her name. Joan glared at me from the top of the stairs. Justice had been sleeping soundly for once, and he wasn't going to settle down again easily.

"Henry," I said, repeating myself until he finally listened. When I had his attention I paused a moment, then said, "I think you'd better not call me anymore."

Henry didn't answer. A heard a bottle move, a glass fill, but I didn't hear Henry drink. There was a pitiful echo of Justice coughing while he bawled. I wanted Henry to tell me

1

to eat shit and die. If he was going to straighten out, I wanted him to show me he had enough rage to go all the way and shut up anyone who doubted him. Silence, on the other hand, was unbearable. Joan got tired of waiting and went to put Justice down herself.

I told Henry, "Just don't call me anymore."

For a moment, I thought Henry called me an asshole, but he was only sighing.

"Henry?" I said. "Are you listening?"

Henry coughed, then again. Slowly, he apologized ("Sorry, Doug.") and hung up. Had I believed in my brother, I would have called right back and laid into him until he was determined to get sober just to piss me off. Had Henry believed in himself, he would have punched redial and chewed me a new one. Instead, I stared at an inanimate phone while Henry, no doubt, was doing the same.

Somewhere among Justice's screams I could make out Joan's voice, reduced through the walls to an unintelligible murmur. Joan couldn't sing well except when she sang to Justice. I went upstairs and lingered in the hall so I could hear Joan's voice more clearly—so low, so kind and warm. I took in the smells of the central heating. When I turned off the living room light from the top of the stairs, I was sure for a moment that someone was still down there, looking up at me from the recliner. I could have helped Joan quiet the baby, but instead I went to bed and lay down.

When Joan came back to bed an hour later, I was still awake. I told her what I had said to Henry, and she was stuck, it seemed, between congratulating and chastising me. Eventually, she asked, "You told him never to call again?"

I was not supposed to answer. Joan was giving herself time to find a way of consoling me, but I didn't want consoling, and she put her head on my chest.

When I was fifteen, Henry got me served in my first bar. Before that, we'd finished off bottles of blackberry brandy or Southern Soft together under the boardwalk and behind electric factories, but at the Hi-Point Inn we found a pair of bar stools that stuck to us like barnacles. By the time I was sixteen, Henry nineteen, we were regulars, the Boyle Brothers, the Boilers to some, but no one believed we were related. I was a tall and skinny redhead, Henry an out-of-shape John Cusack. Mom must have known we were coming home drunk almost every night, but she wasn't one to make a scene. She was only head of household because Dad had died in his sleep when I was ten, and she never took to the position very well.

Dad had served in Vietnam as a radio specialist. He didn't even meet Mom until they were both in their forties, and neither seemed comfortable with children. Mom always held back her anger, as though we'd break if she punished us, and Dad merely shook his head when we violated the code of conduct and expectations he never explained. After his death, Mom started filling every available space in the apartment with knickknacks she bought by the crateful: *National Geographic* arranged in collectible boxes, piggy banks from around the world. Seasonal items stayed out year-round, since there was nowhere left to store them. She fed every cat in the building and took in strays. She fed squirrels and seagulls. When Henry dropped out of high school, she told him hard work, not education, makes success. I moved into a vo-tech program when I flunked everything but woodshop, and she told me in warm tones that I needed to focus on a craft. She was more willing to yell at the cats for knocking over one of her plug-in ceramic Christmas trees than raise her voice at us.

Henry and I stayed on at Mom's until I was twenty-one. We snuck money from her purse or bureau when we needed it, or we sold some of the glass figurines that occupied the tables and shelves in thick hordes. We got jobs mopping the floors and urinals and putting out the trash at the Hi-Point when all we could get out of Mom anymore were handfuls of loose change. On my twenty-first birthday, Henry and I moved into a motel room within walking distance of the Hi-Point and some other dives we liked. Mom didn't help us pack our bags, but she didn't stop us, either. She told us we should stop by for dinner on Sundays and that our beds would always be vacant.

For five years Henry and I moved in and out of cheap rooms and holed up with temporary girlfriends. Getting fired was more important than finding a job, especially if we got canned for pissing on a tray of fried chicken or getting favors from a teenage coworker. If I had to hide from a landlord or sleep in a car for a few days, I had a story to tell at the bar. The closer we were to disaster, the more Henry and I thought we were enjoying ourselves. Still, every other Sunday, Henry and I went to Mom's for takeout pizza and a round or two of Parcheesi. We were usually in bad shape, if not bruised or marked up from a fight or former squeeze, but Mom still acted like it was a holiday. She'd tell us again about Dad teaching her to play skeeball and the time Henry tore into a box of Quaker Oats when he was a baby and threw it around like it was the best toy ever invented. Henry and I would slam back her iced tea as though momentum could generate a little kick to it, and Mom would push some cash on us before we left.

It was no singular event that convinced me to dry out. I had slept next to my own puke on a curb several times, and getting beaten down by someone who had more friends than I had bargained for was a semi-annual tradition. I got twenty bucks a pop to start the coffee and unlock the doors at a VFW before the evening advocacy groups convened. I got a little extra if I stayed and mopped the main hall, so I eavesdropped on the Anonymous meetings. At first, I listened for funny stuff to tell Henry later, and hell, I wanted to check out the female addicts who screwed as voraciously as they drank. After a while, I listened in to remind myself how misguided the advice touted at these meetings was. One of the regulars, a hairy column of a man who used to ride with the Pagans, talked as though sobriety were a 12-year campaign for the Holy Land. "Don't sweat the battles," he'd say. "Just win the war." The gangly zombie who brought the handouts and constantly sucked on cinnamon candy told the blubberers and the vow-breakers that it was okay to fall off now and then, a thousand times even, as long as they renewed their commitment the next day. I wanted to snap the mop handle and shove the splintered end into his face. The twelve steps were bullshit. My program was going to be direct and uncompromising, and it could be described in two words: That's It.

I saved up a hundred dollars and took a bus into the Pine Barrens. I found a house that rented rooms and signed on at a Popeye's buttering biscuits, changing syrup kegs and emptying the deep fryer. I never told Henry or Mom where I was going. My place was so tiny I had to do my push-ups in the hall. At night, I thrashed on the bed and sweated for a drink, but I was going to prove those AA pussies wrong. I had a contract—if I ever let myself drink again, I was going to drink until I was dead. No glacial progression, no one day at a time, no forgiveness. I was going to stay dry, or I was going to choke on my own blood on a cracked sidewalk. In seven years, I went from fast food minion to bank teller to executive assistant to the manager of the loans department at an Ocean City Savings. I met Joan in a bookstore—she was reading a biography of Lisa Marie Presley while I laughed out loud at a volume of Deepak Chopra. Finally, I showed up unannounced on pizza night, Joan bulging with our imminent son. Mom danced as much as her bad feet let her, and Henry looked as though I were wearing a flounder on my head.

On the phone that night, when Justice was supposed to be sleeping, Henry was nothing more than another self-pitying sop looking for someone to encourage him out of his hole. What he got was a fire hose on full blast. I had given Henry two options: abandon his lair for the frigid winter of a new life, or drown.

That weekend, Mom called and filled me in on the details. Henry had found a bargain house that needed work to make it barely habitable. His new girlfriend, Sarah, had a daughter. This made Henry a family man in Mom's eyes.

"Margot's such a good kid," she told me. "Henry showed me pictures. He has big plans. You should hear all the things he's going to do. You know how handy he is. Sarah's going to help out too, what I hear."

"That's great Mom," I said. "How are your cats?"

The only loan Henry could get was with a mortgage company that advertised on late-night television. Mom gave me weekly reports. Henry replaced the water heater and patched the roof. He put up a swing set in the backyard. He insulated. When I got tired of listening to Mom drone on, I handed the phone over to Joan, who got to hear the whole diatribe again from the start. I wanted to see Henry pull off a new life, but the shopping list of house repairs proved nothing. Ten years ago, if you had told me that I would one day have a kid and a job in a bank, I would have laughed in your face and shoved you off your stool. Henry was a little more set in his ways, but I couldn't help listening for hints that he was going to pull this off.

With the weeks came omens of failure. Henry stopped working on the house. Mom defended him because Henry was now a high school custodian, night shift, and he slept all day.

"He must be swamped," Mom explained, "cleaning up after those kids."

Then Margot got a black eye from falling off a table at her day care, and Sarah wanted to switch her to a more expensive program. There were fights over money. Henry lost his custodian job, and soon he was drinking every night. Two months after Henry and Sarah moved in together, Henry came home drunk and found the locks changed. He punched through a window on the side door to let himself in, and Sarah beat his arm back with an imitation fireplace log.

Mom called the day Henry was supposed to move out. I was waiting for dinner. Joan was in the kitchen. Justice was sucking on an empty baster.

"Henry's moved most of his stuff here already," she told me. She sounded harried. I could picture her pacing as far as the phone cord would let her, one of the cats watching her from a nearby perch. "He's got just a couple more trips to go, but he can't get the love seat in his car. I can call when Henry gets back here, and maybe you two can meet at the house and bring the love seat over together." This was the closest to a direct order I'd ever heard from Mom. Either she was exhausted from moving Henry's stuff around all day, or Henry had been nagging her to get me to lend a hand. Maybe she was just fed up with the both of us. I told her I could maybe spare and hour and wrote down the address.

"Henry's moving in with Mom," I told Joan. She wiped her hands on her apron and waited for the inevitable more. Justice pointed the baster at her, and she took it from him.

Finally, I explained that I was going to take the minivan and help Henry move a thing or two.

"The man you never want to talk to again?" When Justice whimpered, Joan wiped spit from the baster and gave it back to him.

"He's my brother, already," I said. Even I knew it was just an excuse.

The first I saw of Henry as I came up the street was his shit-brown Chevette. It was packed to the ceiling with cardboard boxes and duffel bags, the hatch roped shut. The neighborhood consisted of old one-story houses. Paint was peeling, and children ran without shirts on overgrown lawns. Henry paced along the gutter before his dream house. He was dressed in jeans and a rumpled flannel shirt with the sleeves rolled down to hide the wound on his forearm. The Yankees cap was only just able to contain his dark curls. He still favored his left leg from when he lost twenty dollars on a game of pinball against some college kids and refused to pay. Band-Aids on his right hand covered the first two knuckles. He was out of breath, though he tried to hide it as I pulled up in the minivan.

"Doug," he said as though he were trying to remember my name. It was reassuring to see Henry so down, so beaten. I got to feel magnanimous, a saint in a yellow Arrow shirt and loafers. There was no doubt I was the better man. Henry offered no apologies, no sign that our last conversation ever took place—he needed my van, and we were going to tolerate each other until the job was done.

"That sofa inside?" I asked, motioning toward the house. The front windows were covered with insulating plastic. A loose corner snapped loudly with a sudden breeze. There were no other cars parked nearby, so I assumed that Sarah and Margot were out. Henry poked his cap toward the back of his head, and I made for the house. He told me to go around to the side door.

"The front one's warped," he explained from behind me. "The replacement was going to come soon," he started but did not finish.

The empty window in the door by the handle was covered with a purple cereal box. The door itself was unlocked, and I let myself into the living room, which seemed to take up half the house. The inside felt damp and smelled of wet wood and boiling pasta.

Henry had fallen behind, so I was left alone to face Margot and Sarah. Margot was between two and a half and three, her fine, blond hair pulled into pigtails. She ran a plastic fire truck as though determined to wear grooves into the floor. Her white stockings had a run on the left knee, and Winnie the Pooh reached into a jar of honey on the front of her dress. Sarah sat with her back to me on a sectional sofa. She faced the television, ignoring or despising my presence. Brown, curly hair hung to her shoulders. A silent episode of *Gilligan's Island* lit the room. I wanted to call Joan, to tell her I was at Henry's already, about to load the plush, orange love seat that faced me from the middle of the room. I wanted to tell her I was halfway home.

Margot puckered her lips inquisitively when she looked up at me. I grinned and didn't show any teeth. That I had nearly been Margot's uncle didn't put me at ease.

"Is that your fire truck?" was all I could manage. Just as Margot began to move her lips against each other, possibly about to guess who I was, Henry entered. Margot looked away from me and beamed at Henry.

"Hi," she yelled, and as Henry put his hands on his hips and evaluated the love seat, Margot again yelled, "Hi," as if this were a word she had only recently learned. She let go of the fire truck and reached out to him.

"Hey there, Squirt," Henry mumbled as he turned and scanned the door we had come through. Satisfied with the looks of things, he reached down and lifted Margot by the armpits. She squeezed his neck, then put the tip of her finger on his collarbone and said, "Hen-wee." Henry smiled at her, then looked at me as though embarrassed that Margot had not called him Dad. Margot mispronounced his name again, and Henry let her down. She fell to her backside and pointed at me.

Henry positioned himself at one end of the love seat and looked over at the back of Sarah's head. Maybe he was hoping to see her tremble with anger—some indication that his leaving meant something to her.

Margot pointed at me again, this time with insistence.

"His name's Doug," Henry answered, not looking away from Sarah. "He's Doug."

"Doug," Margot said. Her face went sour, as if the name tasted terrible. "Doug."

"Hi, Margot."

Margot pressed her finger to Pooh's left ear. "Squir-t," she said, spitting a little on the last letter.

Henry squatted by his end and grabbed the love seat from underneath. "Let's get this thing out of here," he said, a statement only in part intended for me.

The love seat was a monstrosity of furniture, overstuffed and bursting at the seams. The cushions were thick blocks of foam, one of them marred by a round crater. No doubt...this was Henry's. His head nestled into the crease in one armrest, the back of his knees crooked over the other, his backside sunk deeply into the crater—this was where Henry lounged like a skinned pig, where he pushed his cap over his eyes as Sarah complained to him of drafts and the holes in the walls that he had not yet gotten to. It was here that his changed life fizzled away like a beer belch, and it left him hiding bruises on his arm caused by a Duraflame log. The love seat was going with him, though, and it was surprisingly easy to carry.

Getting it into the doorway took some work though because I didn't know how to move furniture, and the orders Henry barked to me as he backed his end out were unintelligible. Margot stared at us as we wiggled the love seat between the jambs. Halfway through, it wedged itself in so tight that it stayed put when Henry let go. Henry rubbed his cheek and stared at the love seat as though waiting for it to reveal to him the best way to solve this dilemma, but I snapped. I felt as though I had woken up behind the wheel of a submerged car, the air around me suddenly thick and dangerous. I put my forehead against the armrest of the love seat, and I could feel the upholstery heating. I pushed at the love seat again, but it was packed in there like cannon shot. I was ready to take an axe to it if it kept me much longer in this house full of failure.

I turned to Sarah, who sat with her arms spread like some mysterious deity hiding its face from mortals. It had its hand on the valve that would pump in enough air for me to live on, but first I had to offer an oblation, convince it of my worthiness. I wanted to tell my whole story, my dregs and revision, to that curly head and wait for it to nod and affirm my existence, or shake and pulverize me with a heavenly rock. I hadn't felt such a brick in my gut since sweating out the shakes in my quart-sized apartment in the Pine Barrens, when the smell of my own deep-fried hands doubled the retching I did into the toilet while my body tried to convince me to throw back a mouthful of Jagermeister, Gordon's, anything that would settle this craving for the moment. Had the back of Sarah's head disapproved of me, I would have abandoned everything. Joan, Justice, the bank—all of them would have been staring down at an empty hole, which would stink with the smoke of immolation.

But when Henry said, "We have to push it back inside and try something else," I took a step back for leverage, then threw my shoulder into the side of the love seat. I was going to decide the outcome of this trial. This would be my test of worth, a test of my own efforts and not of my past. No ex-girlfriend of Henry's was going to stand in judgment over my worth. This fucking love seat was going through the door.

Henry pushed on his end of the love seat, but I answered with a push of my own, so hard that I heard material tear a little, but the love seat budged.

"Whoa, tiger," Henry said, but I pushed again, damn the tearing fabric, because there was no going back, and that was what Henry wanted. Back with Mom, back to drinking, back to stealing quarters from Mom's change box.

"There is no back," I said, thrusting myself against the love seat every other syllable. I could have told him that going forward, even if the forward path held only desiccation and misery, was the only option, but I said only, "Go forward… through…you fuck."

When the love seat seemed ready to clear the doorway, Margot pulled at my pant leg. I tried to ignore her, but she ran her truck into my shoe.

"Juice," she said, the word sounding more like 'deuce.'

"Not now, Squirt," I ordered as I pushed.

The fire truck banged up against my shoe harder, threatening to mark my ankle.

"Margot." Sarah's voice was strong and insistent, with a hint of violence. Sarah turned halfway toward me, so I could see her pink-rimmed glasses and a chin that was like a lump of dough stuck below her mouth. She was older than Henry, and she kept her eyes averted from me. She hung one arm over the back of the sofa and made grabbing motions with her hand. Margot walked over to that hand and took it.

Not that I expected Henry to shack up with a retired model, but it was refreshing to see her so plain and mundane and know she would never have been a good judge of my fate. She was too partial, too slanted. She was as disappointed with Henry as I was, and she would have gladly taken the opportunity to dash me to shards had I given her the power to do so.

11

Henry pulled at his end of the love seat, and it finally moved through the doorway. While I struggled to regain my grip, I took one last look at Henry's failed family. Margot moved her thumb to her mouth and murmured, "Juice." Sarah kept her grip on Margot's other hand.

Henry kept his eyes to the love seat as we got it around the house and into the back of my van. He pushed and shoved at it a few times before he looked at me briefly. "Should stay," he murmured, and he closed the hatch. "I'll drive my own car," he said, "so you can go right home after we unload this thing." Then, without explanation, Henry went inside the house for a few minutes. Maybe he went to make sure there was nothing more he could claim as his own, or to say good-bye to Margot. Maybe he fetched her juice.

I imagined this:

Henry entered cautiously, but with enough noise to announce his presence. He felt like an intruder. If Sarah suddenly told him to get the hell out of her house, he would have obeyed immediately.

"Well, that's it," he said to the back of Sarah's head, her demeanor still stolid and silent.

"I can be reached at my mother's if you need me," he said after an intolerable pause. "If I've left anything behind, just call, and I'll come get it." He wanted to say more, but there were no more words. He hoped Sarah would give him some indication of what to do.

Margot looked at the buckles to her shoes, oblivious to the fact that Henry was leaving for good. Henry walked up to her and touched her on the head. He stroked one of her pigtails and said, "I'm going now, Squirt," but Margot only looked up at him and hummed around the thumb in her mouth.

Henry came out quietly, empty-handed and sullen, and went straight to his car. "It's getting on six," he said. "Joan's going to want you home soon."

It was dusk by the time we got to Mom's. While Henry climbed into the van to get behind the love seat, I saw Mom, in her black housedress with faded orange flowers, looking down at us from the third floor. A calico watched us from the same window. Mom didn't wave, and I looked away quickly.

The buzzer to the front door rang before Henry and I reached it. Henry still barked orders as we brought the love seat up the stairs, but they were becoming easier to follow. "Level" meant for me to lower my end. "Go" meant that I was to push forward: I was getting the hang of it.

Mom left the door to the apartment open, and as we entered, she barred Roman, her black and brown tabby, from escaping into the hallway. Roman stared at her apathetically, as though watching the evening news.

"The cat's going to get out," she whimpered, shifting to keep her body in Roman's way. "The cat." She limped slightly from the swelling in her ankles she was reluctant to see a doctor about.

I kicked the door closed behind me. Though Joan and I hadn't been by to visit in a few months, even the smell of mildew, tainted with the odor of cat litter, was familiar. The mantle over the useless fireplace was still clogged with ceramic figurines: ballerinas frozen en pointe, smiling pink and blue humanoids with egg-like heads, leaf-shaped ashtrays. An old photograph of Dad in his army uniform hung above it all. My arms were tired from carrying the love seat, and I asked Mom where we could put it.

She waved off the thought of making a decision. "Anywhere at all," she said. "You can just put this in the dining room, if you want, until we move the furniture around in here some..."

"It'll go," Henry said, pulling his end, and me, toward his room. "I got just the place for it."

Mom still had Henry's old twin bed and bureau, but the rest of the stuff was from Sarah's. There were orange milk crates filled with audiotapes and stereo equipment, pillowcases stuffed with rectangular objects, grocery bags filled with clothes, but there was no room for the love seat. Henry nearly dropped his end twice bringing it into the room.

"We can put it behind the dining room table," Mom suggested cautiously.

"On the bed," Henry said, his voice straining as he lifted his end. "We'll just let it sit here for now."

It fit, though just barely. I backed out of the room as Henry made sure the love seat was balanced. Mom came up behind me and whispered, as though she did not want to disturb a sacred ritual, "You want some iced tea?"

I had to call home. I left Henry admiring his own skills of balance and told Joan that I was going to be home soon. I could hear the television behind her, the sound up to calm Justice, who got grumpy in the early evenings. The applause of a studio audience soothed him.

"Dinner's ready," Joan reminded me. "It's been nearly two hours." Her voice was a pleasure to hear. I longed to see Justice spill his milk on his high chair.

"I'm leaving right away," I told her. "I'll be home in fifteen minutes." Mom came over and waved her hands in the air. She pointed at me, then at the floor. She mouthed the word *you* as she pointed at me again.

You can eat here, she was trying to tell me. *You can stay here and eat with us.*

To leave, to rush out of the apartment without a good-bye or a care that Roman may sneak out behind me, was an act of survival. When Henry was balancing his love seat on top of his childhood bed, his thoughts were obvious—moving back in with Mom was the best thing for him. She wouldn't complain. She wouldn't bug him about getting a job. She wouldn't gripe about empty beer bottles all over the floor. Moving back in was like pretending nothing had ever happened in his life.

I got as far as the playground behind the library before I had to stop. It was the playground where Mom used to take Henry and me, where Henry once cut my head open during a rock fight, where I first got drunk when I was eleven and threw up into the sand by the swing set, Henry patting my back and laughing as I coughed and spat.

The lump in my throat was heavy and painful, but I refused to cry. My job, a marriage, a child—the future was overwhelming in that moment. The playground, with its seesaws and child-safe swings, looked inviting. I could have told Joan that I was caught in traffic, the victim of circumstances beyond my control, just to spend a few minutes sitting on the redwood benches by the stone checker tables.

But I couldn't stay. I couldn't stand still, even for a moment. I wiped off what weren't yet tears and went home. Justice was asleep in his carrier. Joan stabbed me with her eyes, but greeted me warmly with her lips, which tasted of potatoes and lip balm. We didn't discuss my afternoon. She didn't comment on the fact that I didn't eat much.

Mom called that Saturday, but I had Joan tell her I was out. Joan answered Mom's questions about her well-being and Justice's latest antics. She made sympathetic sounds when Mom complained about her ankles, and she promised to have me call as soon as I got back. As soon as she hung up, Joan told me, "From now on, you're back." The next Saturday, when the phone rang, Joan stared me down, but I let it go to voicemail. The message is always the same:

"Hello, Doug, this is your mother. Hope Joan and the baby are all right, and I'll try to reach you again in a little while." She enunciates as though speaking to a near-deaf scribe. Then, as if in afterthought, "Hope all is well."

I listen for signs of Henry in the background. Sometimes he's yelling at the TV or talking baby talk to a cat. I swear I can even hear that he's walking around in his boxers, a beer in his hand. What I'm really listening for is happiness. I tell myself there is no way Henry can be a truly content man, but I'm not certain enough to believe that without evidence. Joan has a hard time looking me in the eye when I'm listening to the message, hates it worse when I replay it two or three times. I know it's a form of shame she's feeling, but I don't know how deep it runs.

Richard Weems

THE EASTER BUNNY EFFECT

I met Jake in a stink-hole dive called The Shining Tap. When I hunkered onto the stool next to him, he pulled on the bill of his cap and nodded as though he had saved the spot from undeserving strangers. Easter was a day away, and Marjorie was keeping Trudy from me for lack of child support—what better time to go on a heavy toot? The Shining Tap was dark, maybe even foggy, and Jake bent so low in his seat he could have snorted his gin. An Orioles cap barely covered his bald spot and skin tumor. Four hours later, we were as tight as twins.

Whether I hovered over a bottle of Mad Dog under the boardwalk, pulled at some Olde English on a bus stop bench, or twiddled my fingers in a bowl of party mix in a dark bar, I sought in those days the solace of others who also drank and bemoaned their bad luck. I emptied municipal trashcans and drove a truck that I smelled like at day's end. This shit-work barely covered the bills back when I was a married man, but as a divorcé, I had to chip in for my ex's apartment and make due with a box with a communal toilet and shower. While I told Jake my story, he shook my hand every few minutes or so in a hug-warm grip and told me every time that I was all right. He said as he squeezed the blood from my fingers, "Everyone else don't matter, man: you're all right by me."

Behind the spray-painted windows of The Shining Tap, safe from the morning sun, we forged a fellowship out of liquor and common unhappiness. And we weren't alone here, at the ass-end of the world. Around the corner sat an underage Hispanic boy and a pretty, brown girl he bought drinks for. Across, two off-duty prostitutes who drank Remi Martin and broke fifties with each round. One was black with a blond wig, the other Asian, maybe Filipino. They were streetwise and chisel-faced and kept their chins up so nobody could make eye contact with him. And up by the wall was a drunk who knew every Three Stooges film by heart. To get another Rolling Rock from the bartender, he called out, "Hey, porcupine," with the curt insistence of Moe, the bossy Stooge. Dennis, the bartender, wore a striped pullover that called attention to his belly. His blond and silver mustache pulled his face down. Dennis could have put Jake and me out on our ears long ago, but we were harmless-enough looking drunks. We didn't spill our drinks often, and we kept our money in an empty nachos basket as proof we could pay our tab. Every time Jake sipped his bar gin with a squirt of soda he managed to leave a little more in his beard.

I told Jake how I had blown off my support payments to tell Marjorie she had no control over my life anymore. She threatened to keep Trudy from me altogether, so I left long, angry messages on her phone: "Pick up, damn it, pick up for Christ's sake, damn it, pick up the damn phone, I know you're there, so pick up the fucking phone." Trudy was four, and for almost half of her life I had been little more than an occasional babysitter who cut her pizza into thumb-thick rectangles. In my room, I kept a stuffed pink bunny, some alphabet blocks, a Hungry Hungry Hippos game and a lawn mower/vacuum cleaner that popped colored balls into a dome when Trudy ran it along the floor. Trudy got bored with most of these within a few hours of being over, but a larger toy cache would have looked too much like a shrine to a missing child, so I let her watch a lot of TV.

But I was going to become a proper dad come Easter—I had a foolproof itinerary. We would see the Easter Bunny, the real thing, so she could sit on that fuzzy, pink lap. Then she would come back to my place to a basket full of chocolate and Peeps bedded down among some plastic eggs and grass. Ham and mashed potatoes for dinner, all the butter and salt she wanted. And hell, if she wanted to open a can of grated cheese and dump that all over her plate, I would let her do exactly that. Maybe she would have given me a squeeze around the neck and begged me to stay a little longer when I told her it was time to take her back to her mother's. But if Marjorie kept Trudy from me, my little girl was going to forget that she even had a dad.

Jake shook my hand. "I'm with you, man," he said, and I believed him.

Jake was a learned man. He had studied sociology and the British Romantics at Tuscaloosa. He had come to Atlantic City to make his fortune, work his system, but within hours the Trump operatives grabbed his cash, his watch, his gold necklace, and his bus ticket home, so he moved into a water heater crate behind a skeeball arcade. He grew heroin-thin; his eyes widened into cereal bowls of fear, his cheeks into misshapen prayer stones inside leather pouches. An ambush by lifeguards left him with a bad gimp. It took him months of panhandling, selling plasma and pushing fat tourists around the boardwalk on rolling chairs to earn the money, but Jake developed his own business. He sold postcards, fake dog shit and hot pepper gum, though he didn't have a permit and had to work out of a suitcase.

"I can pull in forty dollars on a good day," Jake said. "I live in a room the size of a litter box, and I eat ravioli straight from the can. And for this, I'm supposed to feel blessed." Jake tapped his temple. "I know a thing or two about being blessed, pal, and I'm no pope."

"Damn straight," I said, and I threw back another Clan MacGregor for punctuation.

From there, Jake and I discussed anything worth philosophical discourse: the rationale behind the shapes of martini glasses, the intricacies of Sumo wrestling, the necessity of dollar coins. When we meandered back to the subject of our hardships, Jake suddenly grew angry and hammered the bar with his fist.

Our glasses rattled. All conversation muted. A moment of tense silence except for the Spanish guitar on the jukebox.

"I did that because I wanted to, man," Jake said, "because I'm no cow. No way I'm a cow. Do I look like a cow?"

I shook my head. "This ain't no dairy farm," I said, and I looked around, daring someone to contradict Jake. For a moment I thought the Hispanic boy, trying to impress his date, was going to say something smart. Had that boy said anything like, "You *do* look like a cow. A skinny, ugly cow with a lump on your head," I would have turned on him and gotten in a few licks before anyone could have pulled me off.

"No, man, I ain't no cow," Jake said. Dennis watched us as though we were in a low-quality television pilot. The Three Stooges drunk blurted out, "Moe, Larry, cheese! Moe, Larry, cheese!" Jake's hairy mouth hypnotized me.

"Do you wait in line to go through only one side of a set of double doors?" he said. "Or do you push open the other door your own damn self?"

I wanted to push open the other door my own damn self. The bunny I kept for Trudy's visits was an old one, and sometimes I held it to my face to catch a whiff of her. It wasn't right that Marjorie should keep this bunny from her. Trudy loved bunnies—Peter Cottontail, Bugs, Winnie's Rabbit. She gawked at them in book store windows, kept a horde of them on her bed at home. If I asked her during our visits what bunnies did, she'd say, "Hop!" and she'd hop once or twice, and so I'd ask again and she'd hop again. We sang bunny songs while she hopped, songs that we revised to make them all about bunnies, "The Hopper in the Dell" and "The Bunnies on the Bus," and she smiled at me as though I was her favorite person. Trudy deserved to have as many bunnies as she could get, and I was just the mutherfucker to get another one of her bunnies back to her.

"The bunny," I said, meaning not just the bunny I wanted to sneak back into my daughter's arms, but the Bunny whose lap I wanted to sit her on, and every bunny in the world that I could pile onto her little bed. When I said, "The bunny," I also meant my daughter, my little hop-a-dee-hop-hop bunny, but when I said, "The bunny," Jake's eyes caught fire with the napalm of a devastating plan.

He grabbed me by the shirt and said, "Let's go get that shit-ass, that Easter Bunny, and let's beat his pink balls into the ground."

A keen rage fired up in his eyes. I tried to explain, tried to say that I was going to make Marjorie take that damn stuffed bunny back, but Jake had his hooks deep into an idea that he wouldn't shake.

"He's just blocks from here, man," he said. "I saw him yesterday and you know he's going to be there today and it's time. It's time, man, you know it's time."

Jake's intent could have been tattooed on the bridge of his nose. Jake wanted us to unload our frustration on some loser pulling minimum wage in a humiliating suit. No doubt, the target deserved a good beating—that forced smile and militaristically happy pink Dacron fiber—but it was a bunny after all, an object of my daughter's affection and fascination, so I rose up like a bull making a last stand against a shiny matador.

"No way," I told Jake. "You drunk. You bum. Get off me." I balled up a fist and made like I would deck him if he got any closer.

Jake deflated a bit, his longtime compadre of six and a half hours now his opponent.

"Don't you worry none," he said as though in consolation. "They'll kill me and they'll stretch out my skin in the sun, but I'm going to die for you anyway." His eyes went from hot to sloshed, and any semblance of rational thought dissipated. I shrunk from his glare and looked into my scotch.

Jake turned and left with a war cry, something like a belch with teeth.

Dennis took away Jake's empty glass and soggy coaster. "You sure you don't want to be leaving with your friend?" he said.

I took the hint readily. "I'd better get out there, then," I said, and I offered up the money Jake had left behind. I convinced Dennis to sell me a pint of Clan MacGregor for the road.

The next day, Easter, everything turned black.

The article on the back pages of the local section was four inches long at best: "Easter Bunny Bopped." Just hours after my whirlwind friendship with Jake, a supposedly unknown assailant worked over the Easter Bunny at the mall just a few blocks from The Shining Tap. A line of sticky-faced kids watched while the Bunny got kicked and slapped around, and they continued to watch as the Bunny was carried away for overnight observation. The perpetrator ran off before security could come down on him.

"It's hard to understand what makes someone go and do something like that," quoth the Easter Bunny's assistant, a fuzzy chick who hadn't lifted a wing to help.

I read the article while I swigged back some orange juice. Clan MacGregor still washed along the lower edge of my vision, and I laughed the story off at first. That crazy bastard Jake. Then I called Marjorie for a time to pick up Trudy, and she didn't answer. I called again, and when her voicemail again asked me to leave my name and number, I hung up and sent a string of texts (when? When?? WHEN?!?), but still no reply. I took a cab to the apartment building. The brown cabbie kept tabs on me through the rearview as though I were a fugitive.

I rang Marjorie's apartment three times. Still nothing. The building foyer was small and smelled of boiled turnips. I rang Marjorie's neighbors, but they also denied me entry. I broke a sweat that was pure liquor. With each doorbell I pushed, I felt the sphere of Trudy's life floating away from mine. There was no credible way to think my little girl could have known that I had had something to do with the attack on the Bunny, but rationality was the last thing on my mind.

When I snuck in behind a flower delivery and heard the sounds of television and a running sink behind Marjorie's door, I pounded and got no answer and pounded and pounded. Neighbors threatened through their doors to call the police, but fear didn't let me stop. Little Trudy screamed while I shouldered the door again and again. I should have walked away and straightened out the matter later with a cooler head, but I was ready to take a splinter through the neck rather than deal reasonably with the notion of losing my own daughter. I was ready to bleed to death on the floor of Trudy's bedroom rather than be shut out of her life.

Soon came the authorities and the trip downtown and the writing of reports. I even confessed to bringing down the hit on the Easter Bunny, but without a last name, the police had no hope of catching Jake. The ordeal ended with a restraining order and an edict to attend counseling for any hope of reinstating visitation privileges, but I didn't need experts with trained superiority telling me shit. All I needed was to set the record straight with Trudy, so I parked myself in the garbage heap in the alley across the street from her apartment building and waited for a chance to tell her the true story. I sealed the stuffed bunny in a Zip-loc to keep it free of stink. This mission became more important than work, than getting home to shower, than paying rent. A homeless shelter sat just a short walk away, and there were plenty of suckers in the world willing to shell out some loose change for a poor drunk. In the morning, I watched Marjorie drag Trudy to the bus stop in the morning and drag her back in the afternoon. Trudy's knit hat was always twisted as though forced onto her head, her frown crinkled and powerful. Marjorie, that Cerberus with a poodle-like perm, never left the girl alone for a minute.

I saw Jake once more. This was early June. I was outdoors by then, a dirty semblance of the broken man I once was. Jake sold tiny airplanes on a street corner. He wore a grimy shirt and a paisley clip-on. The box he sold out of looked as though it had fallen from a truck. These airplanes looped in the air and always came back to him. I avoided meeting eyes with him—he probably wouldn't have recognized me, and I was still hopeful at the time I would someday talk to Trudy, so I shambled by.

And then, a few weeks later, I heard through the shelter grapevine that Jake was dead. He had choked on a roast beef end on the curb in front of a convenience store. No one slapped his back or called for help. No one took note of the carcass until the owner tried to prod him awake with a giant Pixy Stick. No one at the shelter knew his name, but word had it the guy was skinny and bald, a lump of skin cancer on his forehead.

If the breeze off of a butterfly's back can eventually stir up a hurricane, what chance does an old drunk have when he goes and kicks the Easter Bunny's ass? It was impossible not to think that Jake's crime against the Easter Bunny had come back at him like a divine boomerang. And if that was indeed the case, how could anything but disaster wait in the wings for the guy who unwittingly put him up to it?

Just a couple of months after the news of Jake's death, I got my chance at Trudy.

She snuck downstairs one Saturday morning. Marjorie was probably sleeping off her waitressing shift. Trudy had on Beatrix Potter footed jammies, a bunny slung over her shoulder as though it were a bindle. She fingered the borders of the lobby mailboxes as though she were scratching at the paint on the Mona Lisa. My little girl was tense with the thrill of escape.

Of course, I moved too quickly. I was too excited. I was too sober. I hadn't had a liquor fix since a honk or three of some Old Crow with some hag at the shelter the night before. I emerged from my garbage pile like Godzilla from the sea, the bagged bunny dangling from my claws, and I tromped across the street towards her. I entered the foyer with a flourish, my crusty clothes crackling with various forms of energy. With only security glass between us now, the closest we'd been since I had shouldered down her front door, I must admit that I was too eager to close the distance, and I lurched at the glass.

The girl was scared shitless, and she had every right to be. Trudy scampered back into the stairwell, away from the heap on two legs that offered up a shit-brown baggie.

That night was when I started dreaming about the Easter Bunny. I'd be back in my old apartment, alone, when he'd burst in through the window by my bed, straddle my chest, and have at me with shiny, adamantine claws. After struggling briefly against his indomitable strength, I would let my arms fall from my face and ask for forgiveness and the sparing of my eyes.

"Too late, too late," he'd scream through his mask. His voice was deafening. Enough to wake me, fortunately.

Marjorie and Trudy must have moved out one evening while I cruised the boardwalk for tourist alms and stale caramel corn. I held out against despair and kept vigil morning and night for a few days, but neither of them appeared again.

There is another woman I watch now. She may be a hairdresser, or a manicurist. She wears a pink smock under her jacket, and her perm is wide enough to hide a shih tzu. She has a girl a year or two older than Trudy but a worthy vessel just the same. The girl sometimes comes home with her shoes unbuckled, her jacket a little rumpled. Maybe she's getting bullied at school. If she is, I hope she's taking her lumps and learning a thing or two about life. Watching them come and go is as satisfying as a long pull on some rot gut bought with someone else's spare change: a burn, then a lingering, acrid cloud in the nose, then a dull rush to live on for a little while.

Richard Weems

A MEMORIAL FOR HAMMERHEAD

Bad enough it had to be a rhino like Hammerhead, a fighter who at forty-seven could still hold down solo one of those high-yield elephant trunk hoses that sprayed gallons by the heartbeat. We knew fighters who went down in the Towers, and they had their names carved into brass and stone, but Hammer went out in a lame-ass way and didn't get any such remembrance. He came off the ladder after a routine blaze at an apartment house. He was spraying down the remains of the roof, his safety line not hooked properly. I guess we all make mistakes, but I had a hard time feeling something other than a gyrating anger that Hammer had to go out like a granite-headed rookie and leave Meg, Danny and me to make a go of it without him.

The fighters who came for the service had on their game faces. They looked like they were attending a mandatory staff meeting—dutiful, but wanting clearly to be out barbecuing on a day like this. Meg, Danny and I knew where they were coming from. We three were the closest thing to surviving family, but no one looked to us to say anything. We sat in the back like pewter-cast figures. I could barely even look at Hammerhead, his hands folded over his chest as if someone were holding him down for the three-count. The chief brought out his usual platitudes about duty, and then we were made to stare at a radio as it played "Ghost Riders in the Sky." Danny's metal joints clinked rhythmically during the chorus. When it came time to pay respects, I stayed where I was. I could think of nothing new to say to the rat bastard.

But Meg thought differently. "Here we go," she said and got up. As she joined the line that had formed in the aisle, Danny tapped my leg with his flask. One of the fighters in front of us, a volunteer from Hamilton Township, turned back and gave me a brief, knowing nod. Like hell I was going to offer him any whiskey. And I didn't need his damn permission to get lit at a buddy's funeral.

When Meg's turn came, she strode past the casket as though she just wanted to make sure it was Hammer crammed in there and not some other thick-necked slob in a dark blue uniform. As she walked back up the aisle, she bowed her head to keep her sun-bleached curls in her face and avoid eye contact with anyone else. When she sat down, Danny murmured, "Worse than a high fucking school graduation."

"Feel any better?" I said.

Meg scratched her nose boxer-like. "Anything to make this crap go by a little faster," she said.

As soon as things came to an end, the three of us made a hasty exit and manned Danny's pickup. I needed air and crashing waves and a wide fucking berth. I needed beer with sea air mixed into it. Anything to make me forget the funeral parlor smell of stale antiseptic. Danny gunned the engine, took his arms off, and we shot out of the parking lot.

"I feel like I have just taken a major dump," Danny said, his left stump controlling the wheel from the gap over the horn. He flipped on his blue lights, and we charged forward with little regard for the rules of the road. "Another minute in there, and there would have been a system-wide meltdown of global proportions, I shit you not." He swerved among traffic, barely slicing past cars that had only just started to yield.

"It was close in there," Meg said. She sat in the middle and bumped up against my shoulder every time Danny banked left. "I want to say those things never get any easier, but that's not it. I think they've gotten too easy to get through, if that makes any sense."

"I just have a hard time distinguishing one service from another," I said. "It's like I've been looking at the same wallpaper every damn time." Even as I said it, I knew it was a lie. I was going to forget my birthday before I forgot the sight of Hammer squeezed into that box. In that moment, my anger at Hammerhead became so intense I could have torn the upholstery from the cab ceiling. Fighters died, fighters got injured beyond belief, and some took years to cough the rest of their lives out of them. The survivors were supposed to keep doing the job despite the fallen, or because of them. Hammer was gone, and I just wanted to stop everything so I could slap him around for being a careless son of a bitch.

"Open road, bad-ass." Danny shouted encouragement to his truck as small avenues opened up among the cars. The exposed electrical cables at a four-alarm ten years ago that had taken both of Danny's arms just below the elbows had only deepened his need for speed, and today of all days there was a craving for close shaving. I stuck my head out the window and howled into the wind. The wind blew my voice right back into my face.

It was a beautiful day, breezy and warm. We were headed for the North End, the tip of the island, the outer rim of the civilized world. A good place to get primal and pretend away a lot of bad shit.

At the entrance for the beach, state signs mandating only off-roaders with permits, Danny raced for the g's, cut a severe left and kicked up a Sahara dust cloud as we curved onto the tire path. Meg slid into me.

"Whoa," she said. She used my knee to push herself back to the middle. Her hands always surprised me—so small, but managing quite a pinch on my patella as she steadied herself.

We motored past a row of rinky-dink 4X4's parked in the hard sand and kept our sites due north, to the end of the

End, where most every fiberglass import of a jeep or light truck rooted into the deep, soft beach and needed a real vehicle to get it out. Hard not to think of how Hammerhead used to ride on a beach chair in the bed of Danny's truck and raise a beer to the Suzukis and Toyotas.

"We'll be in the deep end," he'd yell, his rump wedged so tightly into the chair that it could have melded with it— Hammer looked like he could get hit by a semi and come up pissed at the driver. "We don't do the kiddy pool," he'd say. "We ain't playing it safe." Atlantic City to the south looked like a row of models fit for a good goddamn Godzilla stomping. Meg and I were already pulling at our uniforms, itching to get down to the bathing suits we had on underneath.

We parked in our usual spot, far enough from the water to account for the tide, and we made motions like it was any other day. Meg helped Danny out of his clothes and put lotion on him. I set up the chairs, opened the beers, and we all had things to do to keep our minds clear until we sat down and stared at the ocean.

The surf was low. The ocean looked like corrugated glass, waves breaking only just on top of the sand. No one but us and some gulls. Every now and then, one of the chairs creaked. Sometimes boaters rode right up onto the beach, but not today. Danny had put one of his arms back on so he could hold his beer. The steel hook gave the can a small, involuntary crunch.

"Think we'll get a call today?" Meg put her beer against her left cheek, then her right.

"Doubtful," I said.

"Only if they really need us," Danny said, "considering. I turned the receiver up just in case."

I looked at the water and thought about how long today would be with Hammerhead's death looming inside of every second. Tomorrow, too. The day after that would still be a struggle, but less so, and so on, the lead ball of doubt, that annoying second-guessing about what you do and whether it is worth the trouble, sinking a little deeper in the sand until it became just another lump I'd be able to travel over again.

Danny stretched and regarded his bare stump. The prosthetic's brace clinked beneath him like a robot out of juice. He bent his elbow, the flesh beneath it smooth and soft and shiny with sunscreen.

"Goddamn," he said. "My nubs hurt. It's like they're getting pinched at the ends."

"Could be you're growing back," I said.

Danny put his beer to his forehead.

"Might make you a better driver," I said. Meg, between us, laughed once.

Danny crunched his beer can, this time with purpose.

And here we were, our conversation in packets, the space between each packet filled with meaningless nods and little eye contact.

"Enough." Meg stood, left behind her beer and sunglasses and made for the water. "I'm leaving the funeral," she called out as she went. The ocean was filled with bright spots of sunlight that moved around as if they were living things playing on the surface of the water. Meg walked in to her elbows before she dove in and started a stroke. Danny and I watched her the whole way.

"She was at that warehouse blaze," Danny said.

I sat up to let sweat roll down my back. "She got called in for that?"

"We all did, bud. Some of us just weren't up to it."

He was right. That blaze was the night after Hammerhead died. Two fighters got inhalation. The kids who started it were trapped inside. News vans all over the place. Not the kind of low drama that took Hammerhead. Danny and I were in no shape to take on that one. We were at Danny's place, drunk. I was talking about getting out, quitting. Who was going to miss Hammerhead outside of Danny, Meg and me? Why the hell was I slowly getting burned to a crisp? But then I had nothing to say when Danny asked, "So what the fuck are you going to do instead?"

"Meg got one of those kids out herself," Danny said as he considered his beer can. "Cut in under the floor, since no one could get an alley sprayed down. Tough as shit, that one." Meg was doing backstrokes. Sometimes her head poked up over the swells, but mostly she was just two arms making arcs in the water.

"Damn," I said. It was something to think about: Meg out there on a call while Danny and I were fumbling drunks over at Danny's apartment; Meg out there doing the job when all I could do was whine about wanting out. "And then she wastes her time with a crew like us."

"Go figure," Danny said. "I have to think sometimes she's keeping an eye on us, not protecting us because I know I'd be a real jerkasaur to anyone trying to mother me."

"I'd hate to see that," I said, though I liked the idea of Meg looking out for me.

"It's more like observing," Danny said. "Like watching a school of mackerel in the shark tank. You can't do shit about the food chain, but it doesn't mean you don't feel bad when nature takes its course."

"Something's keeping her single," I said, "and it's not her looks." I watched those arms as they emerged and dipped back under. I had a thing for her when she was a kid fighter who kicked guys around the kitchen to make sure we couldn't fuck with her. We slept together now and then, usually when we were both drunk, but she never wanted anything more with me. Instead, she married a fighter named Sammy, and then Sammy fell asleep behind the wheel one night and plowed through a Chevette before he stopped dead on a highway divider. Meg never gave me any sign she wanted to pick up with me again, but every time we were out together I waited for her to get that look she used to get.

Danny put both his prosthetics up on the armrests as though he wanted them to get a little sun. "Strong kid," he said. "Hell of a fighter."

I finished my beer and got up. I went down to the water and found Meg among the splashes of sun. Usually she swam hard in long laps, as if in training. Today she was just pushing herself along on her back, her face relaxed. I went out to her, took her in my arms and helped her float. What I liked most about Meg was her calm center, the way she offered composure while us guys got bullheaded or plain-out crazy. A dead husband, one friend fried down to a couple stumps and now another friend dead and good as buried, and she looked as calm as the water we waded in.

Through the water I could see a long, spoon-shaped scar under the deep tan on her thigh. Except for a slight deceleration of her already methodical pace, she gave no hint of noticing me. I guided her around and around in a circle, stretching out my arms to give her as long a diameter as possible. Back on shore, Danny was little more than a tanned smudge in bright green trunks sitting in front of his truck. Meg waved her limbs slowly under the water, her eyes still closed. Perhaps she too was seeing the image of the bad make-up job that had made Hammerhead look more like Ethel Merman.

When the kids pulled up, the three of us were pretty drunk. The kids had to be, too. That, or they were working on it. It was also getting dark. The sun was behind us, but over the ocean it was already night. Atlantic City was lit up, making the clouds glow like God had something to say.

The kids had one of those jeeps that usually didn't make it out this far. Who knows how many times they'd gotten out to push. They had their rap music up high, their KC lights going, and they parked not fifty feet from us. We had seen them coming of course, but who thought anyone else cared to huff it out this far?

Danny had switched arms later in the afternoon, holding his beer in his right now, but when the kids brought their jeep to a halt close enough to light a sand breeze our way, Danny quickly snapped on his other arm and stood. Danny lost patience easily with kids who made a lot of bad noise. Usually it took them doing something stupid or violent before Danny got into it with them, but Danny was a little angry tonight, a little too eager to get pushed over the edge.

"Do they have to pull in so goddamn close?" he said.

"Not like there's much room around here," Meg said.

"Gotta love that music," I said.

All three of the kids wore neon tank-tops, white shorts and baseball caps. All of them had lifeguard tans. Tans from sitting around in a perch waiting for something to happen. They drank from silver beer cans and laughed for reasons none of us knew.

When they turned their music down, Danny called out, "Better be careful, boys. You don't want to go spoiling Daddy's jeep."

The driver was pulling back the top. He stopped and took a few steps towards us. He cupped his ear. "What was that?"

"I'm talking about your Matchbox," Danny said. "They don't do the loop-the-loop so well with sand on the wheels."

The kid nodded and went back. His friends asked him what happened, and as the driver talked his buddies took turns looking at Danny. Danny still faced them. The smile on his face was his forced one, his dangerous one. Danny was looking to make something go down. All he needed was an excuse. Even worse, he may not have needed an excuse at all.

"What's the point?" Meg said. She turned to the ocean again. She was determined not to let the kids disturb her.

"I'm just saying I have no intention of pulling out that Tonka toy piece of shit when it can't dig its own weight into the sand," Danny said to Meg and the driver both. "I'm just saying we were just sitting here. They knew where the fuck we were. I'm just saying it's a big goddamn beach."

The driver of the jeep asked his buddies something we couldn't hear. One of his buddies answered and nodded Danny's way.

"Yeah, that's me," Danny said.

"Let's be cool," I said, but that's something you say when things are already out of control. Danny walked by in front of us and went towards the jeep. I sat forward, ready to back Danny up if I had to. Meg clenched a fist and shook her head.

Danny stopped halfway between the kids and us. "You got something you want to say?"

The driver's friends were the looking types; they could look mean, but they weren't ready to take risks. Those kinds traveled in packs because they didn't know what it was to act on their own. They didn't know what it was like to be cut-off, unsure if your air tank was going to last before someone could get you out, the heat burning you right through your suit. Danny was on his own the night he lost his arms, and even if these kids had known that they wouldn't have given a shit. At least, that's what Danny was probably thinking. The kids shook their heads as Danny held his ground. One, a dirty blond in a pink neon top, seemed to notice for the first time Danny's prosthetics. He looked a little scared now.

The driver himself took a step forward. "Hey man," he said. "We're just here to party."

"So are we," Danny said. "We got a whole cooler." He pointed back towards Meg and me. "We got nowhere to be tomorrow. We can stay out here all night."

"Come on man," the kid said. He was ready to say something else, then he changed his mind. "Are we bothering you? You want us to move man?"

"This is a soft beach," Danny said, "man. But my fucking arms are hurting." He lifted them for emphasis. "I just want to know how you guys got that piece of fiberglass shit down this far."

One of the driver's buddies, the kid in the orange tank who looked like he played defense, went around to the other side of the jeep. Maybe he was just hovering, ready to pack up if necessary, ready to just hang around, ready to join in the fight. The kid in pink, though, was still mesmerized by Danny's arms.

I turned to Meg and put my hand on her shoulder. "Danny's just letting off steam," I said.

Meg released the tension holding her lips together long enough to say, "Him too."

"We can move if you want us to," the driver said. "How about we just move, okay man? We'll just take a spot back down the End a ways." He took out his keys as a peace offering.

Danny turned around. He went right past Meg and me and got into his truck. Meg didn't move, but I got up. Danny started his truck before I could get anywhere close to him, and he pulled around into the jeep's headlights. There, he put the truck in neutral and revved the engine. He turned the blue lights on and off. He leaned on the horn.

"Once up the dune," he yelled out the passenger window. "Let's get that Micro Machine going."

The driver knew better than to do anything but look at the sand. But his buddy the defenseman didn't have the same presence of mind. He came out from the other side of the jeep and taunted Danny. The kid had a jock's fat face. He thought he was indestructible.

Were any of us, Danny, Meg, me, Hammerhead, even Sammy, ever that young?

"Hang it up," he said to Danny. "Hang it up. Give it a rest."

That was all Danny needed. Danny wasn't so drunk as to start off too fast, but he did veer close to the jock on his way upbeach towards the dune. The stupid, stupid jock thought he was too tough for even a drunk driver with no arms in a large-cab Ford and didn't budge an inch.

We all watched Danny motor up to the biggest dune. Meg got up from her chair. Maybe Danny meant to go up near the top and cut back down, but something, probably the beer, made him cut the wheel too soon and too hard, and he tipped. The truck fell onto its right side and slid, front first, back down.

It was crazy. The kids had to be thinking they were dealing with a madman. If throwing your body to the flames as a way of making a living meant being able to go balls to the wall up a dune and picking a fight with a crew of kid lifeguards with little hesitation, then I was in for the long haul. It may not sound like too good a reason, but it was the simple pleasure of it all that really excited me. I cupped my mouth to howl out Danny's name, but Meg cut me off.

"Get him out of there," she screamed.

I turned and looked back at her. It was hard at first to make out her face in the dark, but when I did I didn't know how I couldn't have seen it before. She was horrified. Her eyes, glistening like the ocean, were wide and could have been the actual source of the scream. I had never seen anything like this from her before.

"Goddamn it, get him out of there," she yelled, her hands and head trembling. "Someone's got to get him out of there."

The kids had a head start since they were closer and I was too shocked by Meg's reaction to do anything at first. Even so, they were way faster than me and had some time at the truck before I could get there. Two of them, the driver and the jock, climbed up onto the driver's side and opened the door. The jock held the door up while the driver got down on his knees to fish Danny out. Behind me, Meg continued to yell.

By the time I got to the truck, I could hear Danny cursing out the kid who had reached down inside. The blond kid was standing in front of the underbelly. Without a word, his face all business, he hoisted me up like a pro. Maybe there was some hope for these kids after all.

I got down low to keep the truck balanced. We had to save tipping it back onto its wheels for later. While the jock and driver climbed back down onto the sand, I crawled to the open door and looked down.

"You okay, amigo?"

The only light in the cab came from the dashboard display, but still I could make out Danny wiggling around helplessly against the passenger door. It was a sad sight. His prostheses clanked around unattached and Danny waved his stumps like he was trying to catch a hold of something. "Goddamn it, Jimmy," he said. "Goddamn it. What the fuck, Jimmy? What the fuck? I can't get a grip."

I had a hard time hearing him over Meg screaming. A scary thing, hearing her scream like that. Below me, Danny looked already in the grave himself, the green dashboard display making him a regular zombie.

"Jesus," Danny said. "Jesus. What's with the screeching?"

"That's Meg," I told him.

"I'm fine, for fuck's sake," Danny said. "Tell her I'm in one piece."

But Meg wasn't screaming because of what happened to Danny. She was screaming about everything—Hammerhead, Sammy, Danny's missing arms, all those little pieces that burned off of us every time we went in to do our jobs. When I thought about it, I couldn't imagine what kept her from screaming every minute of the day.

"Let her scream a bit," I said to Danny.

Danny floundered about even more intensely, trying to push himself up, but there was nothing Danny or I could do to help Meg except stay alive for now and give her nothing more to grieve over.

"Stay down, Danny," I said. "Keep still until we can upright you."

"Someone's got to stop her," Danny said. "I don't think I can take much more of this."

I looked up to find Meg and tell her Danny was okay, we were all okay, and we were going to get out this just fine, but I couldn't say a thing when I heard her crying with large, lung-gulping sobs. Night was official, and I could see the jeep and its lights, but Meg was out there in the dark. The sound carried along the beach like an air raid siren. I didn't know if she was still standing or if she was a heap on the sand. The kids and I all looked out into the dark, to the source of misery, all of us clueless as to how to remedy this situation.

"You gotta get him out of there," she wailed.

DANGEROUS LIGHTNING

The man watched from his car as lights turned off and on in the house that used to be his. Maybe that was his ex in the dining room; maybe the boy now lived in the bedroom at the front center of the house. Without binoculars, the man could only guess who stayed in what room anymore. He finished off the Rolling Rock he had smuggled from The Schooner Inn and leaned over the steering wheel to get as close to the windshield as possible. Be a man of your word, the guys at the bar had said, put your money where your mouth is, all that shit. So here he was, gearing himself up to go in. The trees kept his spot a secret as long as he didn't turn on the headlights. A storm was on its way and made the early evening thick with humidity.

The radio announced a dangerous lighting watch until 11:00 p.m.

The man started his car and drove down the road and up the dirt driveway. The bumps, the shifts back and forth, were all familiar of course, but the house was somehow different. The siding was the same, the porch light fixture, too. But there was a change, and he didn't like whatever it was.

He inched up behind his ex's Honda until his bumper tapped hers. He got out and went up the porch steps and through the front door. The door was unlocked. Someone ran into the kitchen as he came in, probably the boy, who should be at least eight now. (How long since he had last come by. A year? Another half?) The living room furniture was in a different order—he couldn't even see the television at first. Jessica had put out a bunch of knick-knacks. They were small, but they caught his eye immediately: tiny, decorative boxes on the lamp table by the door, two on the low shelf in the hall. One announced itself all the way from the living room with its inky, dark red. The man picked up the zebra-colored box by the hall lamp he never liked. The box was heavy and cold for its size—it wasn't even big enough to hold a box of paper clips. He shook it, but there was nothing inside. He pocketed it when he heard Jessica in the kitchen:

"What the hell."

The man went to the living room and sat in the middle of the sofa. By that time, she had come down the hall from the kitchen.

"The hell?" she said. Both of her fists, one in an oven mitt, poked into her hips. She had added on a few pounds; her hair was a little long and out of control.

"Dangerous lightning tonight," the man said. "There's a watch."

Jessica wiped her hands on her work slacks. She had a job typing and answering phones for smart-asses at the community college—he had heard this from Les, a grounds man who hung out at The Schooner.

Jessica said, "Todd," as if only now could she remember her ex-husband's name. A clear insult, that she could for one second forget his name.

"Todd," she said. "Jesus Christ. What the hell?"

"Their words," Todd said. "Dangerous. There's a watch until eleven."

Jessica looked at the clock, no doubt so that Todd would also see that it was barely after seven.

"Their words," he said. Todd raised his hands in futility —the weather was, after all, out of his control.

Liam, the boy, came down the hall. He had a floppy head of hair now, a lot like his mother's. He receded and sat on the bottom two stairs. The girl was no doubt upstairs in her room—teenage girls pretty much lived in their rooms, didn't they?

Jessica took a step to the side, as though about to go back to the kitchen and ignore him completely, but then she settled back into her military-like stance.

"It's a watch," she said. "There isn't any danger. They're just looking to see if anything happens."

"That's a warning," he said. "A watch means there's bad lightning out there and we need to keep an eye out for it."

She shook her head and didn't pursue. But in the end, she seemed unable to help herself.

"That's ass-backwards," she said. She flinched a bit, but Todd only smiled. Jessica said, "The kids have dinner to eat. And then homework." Liam peeked around the corner, and she sent him up the stairs with a look. Before the boy ducked away again, Todd raised his eyebrows at him.

Jessica had done more to the house than rearrange the furniture and add her little boxes. There was a blue border on the living room wall. There were rectangles at random angles as though she had thrown a mass of sponges. But the pattern, if it could be called that, wasn't finished and didn't reach all around the living room. Todd followed it along until it ended, then scoffed and showed her that he was scoffing.

"Ass-backwards," he said, shaking his head at the use of that word. "Like you are with bat versus knife."

Liam crept up past the creaky eighth and ninth stairs and pattered down the upstairs hall, probably to his sister's room to tell her that dad was here. The girl was either going to hole up in her room until dad was gone, or she was going to come down and chew him a new one. No telling which. The girl was fifteen now.

"Bat and knife," Jessica said. She took a quick look up the stairs to make sure the boy was out of hearing range. "Don't start that shit."

Todd pointed at the border. "It's all crooked," he said. "You shouldn't do that stuff by hand unless you know what you're doing."

The guys had made it sound so simple. Les, Billy, Brown Tom and Tips: go there and straighten her ass out, they said. Todd told them how Jessica never listened to him, not once during their marriage, even less afterwards, and they made their solution sound like the easiest thing in the world to do. And here he was, and talking to her was still like talking with a radio show on fifteen-second delay.

Upstairs, a door flew open and hit the wall. Jessica went to the bottom of the stairs as the girl's footsteps trudged across the ceiling. It was the girl who was in the small bedroom now, the one that looked out over the porch. It didn't make sense that a teenager would want a smaller bedroom…unless she used the porch roof to sneak out at night to party and fool around with boys.

"Get that fucker out," the girl said from the top of the stairs. Jessica told her it's okay, just go back and wait.

The house was buzzing now. Things had looked so quiet from the road. Todd put his feet up on the chest that stood in place of a coffee table. No doubt, no one was allowed to do that.

"He goes," the girl said. "You go," she said, louder.

Todd turned his face towards the ceiling, as though this would make him easier to hear. "It's dangerous out tonight."

"Don't," Jessica said. Todd wasn't sure if she had directed this at the girl or him.

The girl paced back and forth. Jessica barred her from the downstairs with upraised hands. Todd heard a creak in the girl's room—Liam, probably, rocking back and forth on a chair or on the floor. Probably still sucking his thumb like a baby, like a little girl. The daughter came back to the top of stairs and yelled, "Just get out, you fuck."

"It's a watch," the girl's dad said. "It's called a watch, Jessica. Means there's danger out there to watch for.

"Your mom has it all ass-backwards," he said to the ceiling.

It took some time for Jessica to get the girl back to her room. She talked in calm tones, said everything was okay, everything. Okay. When the girl did finally stomp back down the hall, she called her dad an asshole and a piece of shit in a voice loud enough to come through the ceiling. Liam was shooed from her room, her door slammed. Liam slunk along the hall and down the stairs slowly, but he stayed out of sight. Jessica put her forehead on one of the balustrades.

Todd took the zebra box out of his pocket and put it on his knee. Jessica looked at the box. Todd moved it to the knee farthest from her.

"You got it all ass-backwards," he said. "Don't you? Watch and warning? Bat and knife? Two choices, fifty-fifty odds, and you always come out on the wrong side."

This was pretty much the same kind of argument he had with her the last time, when he had that floozy Susan with him, Susan who sat on the porch steps and cackled like the drunk bitch she was while Todd and Jessica shouted at each other through the screen door. There was no telling Jessica anything if she couldn't understand something as simple as bat and knife. That night, the argument ended when he turned on Susan and told her to shut her drunk-cunt face. Jessica slammed the front door and Susan tried to make off in his car. It had all been very disordered, very embarrassing. He never got as far as the living room that last time.

"Just don't," Jessica said. "I. The kids have dinner. Just."

"Bat and knife," Todd said. "Tell me which you are."

It was a simple question. You're trapped in a room with someone who wants to kill you, so which do you use to defend yourself: bat or knife? There were only two choices, unless you were a Bruce goddamn Lee, but even a Jedi master would have chosen one or the other.

Todd took the lid off the useless, decorative box. Nothing inside, just as he had suspected. He held up the box to let her see how empty it was.

"Too small," he said, "even for keys. You have some kind of pet ant you want to make a condo for?"

Jessica crossed her arms and looked up the stairs at the boy.

"Knife," Jessica said. "I'm sticking with knife."

She was wrong about this. She was always wrong. Todd had told her over and over, so now she was just determined to be wrong. Since he didn't live in the house anymore, she'd forgotten how much it mattered when she was wrong. Women usually went for knife, but knife was a bad choice, and Todd wanted her to be smarter than other women. Knives were close range weapons, no good for fending off people with bats—hardly anyone ever asked what the other person had.

He shook the empty box to draw her attention to it. "This little shit," he said. "By the door and on the shelves." He threw the box, and it bounced along the carpet like a stone skipping along the surface of a lake. He raised his voice for Liam's benefit. "What the fuck does your mom want with these shitty little boxes, my man?"

Liam didn't answer. There was a boom upstairs from the girl, maybe a bureau drawer falling to the floor. Jessica involuntarily looked up, but no doubt she wanted to act as though the girl wasn't even in the house. Forget the girl. No girl here. That was what Jessica wanted.

Jessica pulled at the oven mitt as though pulling at a boxing glove.

"This little shit," he said. "Everything's wrong with this house, including this little shit you're doing." He sent the lid of the little fucking box after its bottom, only a little harder, and it bounced against the far wall. Maybe the thing was porcelain, maybe ceramic. Either way, it didn't break. Jessica didn't give a fuck about it, even though she had spent who knows how many hours finding this shit and buying it and placing it around everywhere—that lid could have broken, and she would have paid it no mind because she was busy fending off someone who was no better than an intruder to her in this house.

The girl let something else fall upstairs to also let Todd know that he was not welcome, and Jessica stared as though just the right combination of glare and eyebrow curl would send her ex-husband away.

Todd again talked to his son. "You've got the women all to yourself in the house now, my man. They're going to try and change the house and make it like they want it if you don't say something now and then." He dug his heel into the cover of a magazine on the coffee table chest, into a model's fake fucking face. It creased and almost tore, and then he pulled the magazine off the chest and onto the floor. The magazine was as thick as a book and it landed like one.

And Jessica kept staring.

"And get your flabby ass out of the way if you want me out of your fucking house." He looked up at the ceiling and said, "Your fucking house," again, and now he knew the girl was up there crying. She'd probably been crying for a while, because he'd taught her how to cry quietly and she could do so for a while. And now she was crying out loud.

"You're fucking house too, my man," Todd said for his son's benefit. "A house with little useless fucking boxes you can't even put your keys in."

No one listened to him anymore—that much was obvious. The girl was upstairs crying, Jessica a popsicle as she stood between Todd and the stairs that led to the children.

Todd got up and took out his keys to show that he was going. "Remember," he said. "Bat. Stop getting it ass-backwards. Bat is better." At least he had taken her word and used it against her. He crossed half of the living room before he stopped to point at her. He said, "You are going to get someone who knows what the fuck he's doing when you redecorate, aren't you?"

Jessica looked away and didn't answer. The girl thumped around some more, and Todd heard one side of a phone conversation up there.

At the door, he stopped a moment with his hand on the knob and drew in a comforting thought:

He was still a part of this house. Dinner was going to be a quiet affair because of him.

"Go, already," Jessica said. She was mighty, now that Todd was already at the door. He left it open behind him, and she closed it quietly and shut off the porch light, as though she were locking up behind the final customer.

The girl's bedroom light was off, but there she was, at the window, a phone in her hand. A shine of tears at her eyes. Jessica may have put on a few pounds, but the girl had spread out like a parade balloon. He pretended not to notice her when she stuck up her middle finger at him and screamed, "Fuck you, fucker, you fuck," elongating every vowel. He looked at the sky and jingled his car keys. There was still plenty of time to get a drink at The Schooner and tell the guys he'd plopped himself down in the middle of the living room and wouldn't leave until he'd said a thing or two.

Still no rain, but there was lightning in the distance, the accompanying thunder so far away that by the time it reached him it had lost all potency. Pussy thunder. Nor were there any bolts—just clouds lighting up like they were grumbling among themselves, trying to psych each other up to put on a real show.

MASTERBLASTER

When Zoë's dad kicked us out this time, we spent the night under a tarp by the railroad tracks. We shared the few bites of Beef-a-Roni I had in a baggie and some cigarette stubs I kept in a special pocket of my denim jacket. For heat, we cuddled and fooled around. Zoë was small enough that I could button my jacket over both of us. When we couldn't sleep, we stared out at the cold February night and our shitty New Jersey town—two churches, but no free shelter, no soup kitchen, nowhere to go for some charity and a soft, warm place to crash.

Not that we were in any desperate need: come morning, we oozed back into the apartment, our clothes stiff with the smells of cold, cigarette filters and gutter water. Zoë's dad watched TV in his coveralls and didn't give us a slice of his attention. In our bedroom, just a few steps from the front door, we flopped onto the mattress that had grown as flat as a welcome mat. We kept a Greyhound schedule pinned to the wall above our heads—Zoë and I, when we had the money, were going to hop a bus to Durham, North Carolina so we could shack up in a cheap motel and eat fast food, smoke fresh cigarettes and fuck at our leisure. But for now, we had to wait for Zoë's dad and his pig girlfriend to leave for work so we could snatch up some food, poke through the ashtrays and root for loose change. It was usually a few days, sometimes three weeks, before Zoë's dad would give us the steel toe again, but we liked to be prepared.

Zoë put her arms around me and settled into that spot under my right armpit that had been made for her, her chin at rest just above my breast. As cold as she was, her shoulders as rigid as porcelain, her head was heavy with sleep. I went into my pocket for a stub when that trashcan bitch girlfriend started in on Zoë's dad about a stink in the bathroom. I could hear her plastic bracelets clatter along her jiggly forearms as she demanded that at least one room of this fucking place not smell like a litter box.

She said, "You should make the fags clean up their own shit."

Zoë tightened her grip around my chest. "Jesus," she said, and she shivered.

Zoë's dad promptly went into the bathroom and smashed one of his girlfriend's perfume bottles into the sink. While Zoë zipped up her jacket and made motions to me about buttoning up mine, the fat fuck of a girlfriend threw magazines at Zoë's dad, couch cushions, something that sounded like an empty wastebasket. When Zoë's dad tore open a box of her tampons, she swore never to touch his dick again and locked herself in their bedroom.

I waved Zoë off when she reached for my jacket. We'd never been put out on the street two nights in a row. Zoë grabbed some extra clothes from the floor.

Zoë's dad pounded up to our room, but then paused a moment outside the door, maybe to wipe sweat off his forehead or finger back his hair. Somewhere along the way he had grabbed a glass ashtray, and as soon as he shouldered his way in, he pitched it like a fastball. The ashtray pounded into the wall by Zoë's head. Zoë and I moved like electricity. We scrambled past him while he frowned at the dent he'd made in the drywall and the cow girlfriend screamed about his dick size through the bedroom door.

It was when we were outside, pulling on the extra pants and shirts, that Zoë sniffled and said, "That fucking thing landed next to my ear."

I picked up a crushed beer can and launched it at the apartment window. I screamed every curse I could think of in one sentence as though such a spell would turn the can into a lightning bolt. The can clattered on the wall a story short. Still, the effort calmed me down and let me think. We now had a full day and another night to get through, and I had no supplies except for half a package of ramen noodles and three or four cigarette stubs. "Let's warm up at the library," I suggested, figuring we could make a plan for the night from there. Zoë put her arms around my waist, and we walked along like a single creature made from spare parts.

"MasterBlaster, baby," I said, and I squeezed her ass. MasterBlaster was our power word, our mantra during shit storms. While we were together, while we were MasterBlaster, we were more powerful than anything that could break us apart.

The name MasterBlaster came from a movie about survivors of a nuclear holocaust. People lived in a desert, drank water tainted by nuclear fallout and killed each other over camels. MasterBlaster was the collective name for a big, abominable bastard and the midget he carried on his back. Not only were they survivors, but everyone in the movie was afraid to cross them. Zoë wasn't a midget, but she was small for fourteen, and I would have given anything to be a hulking monster that could smash its enemies to rubble rather than a tall, skinny dike with a long face.

To tell the truth, it was Zoë's dad who first equated us to MasterBlaster. Zoë was trying to skulk by him with the ends of a bread loaf he had thrown away, and he pulled her to the TV by the back of her neck and said, "Look, dwarf, it's something almost as ugly as you and your scrawny bitchfriend." We took the name anyway. Fuck his insults—he was going to regret making the suggestion when one day MasterBlaster splattered his face like an egg.

*   *   *

The daytime was easy enough to get through: we sat among the periodicals at the library and took turns napping. We walked around the block a few times when the librarians looked irritated at ignoring us. I made an attempt every now and then to look through a *Rolling Stone*, but mostly I watched Zoë's boots for any sign that she wanted to talk. She didn't, and that was fine with me. As long as she didn't want to cut vents in her arms with some glass or a broken pencil, I could sit around like a dumb mule and wait for her.

Even before I was with Zoë, her dad would kick her out for the night now and then. She'd hole up in the alley among the trash until morning. Once, when she was twelve, Sadie chased Zoë around the streets for an hour. Sadie was one of the regular street urchins and had accused Zoë that night of selling her to Dominicans who whipped her tits with a glass-encrusted belt. At worst, Sadie would have screamed in Zoë's ear for a while had she caught her, but Sadie was a scary bitch —those wide, furious eyes and complicated rape delusions. Sadie was crazy enough to walk right into a church service and scream, "Well, they *really* fucked my pussy this time!"

Our town had only three street urchins, three creatures who spent day and night with nothing to live for but to survive through to the next day. No telling if they had all landed on the street because they were unstable and crotchety, or if they had been decent people once who had been transformed by their bad luck. Besides Sadie, who could have been somebody's oddball sister or aunt, the kind that gets left behind when the family moves, there was Bill, who looked like Professor Plum on the skids. Bill kept mostly to himself, but if we ever holed up in a spot he had an inkling for, he could kick and spit like a wild man. And then there was Preacher Man, the skinny crooked geezer in black slacks who referred to himself in the third person. Preacher Man was a vulture, the kind who pestered his marks until they caved in or knocked him to the pavement. Food, smoke, cash, hand jobs—Preacher Man pestered anyone he targeted for anything he could get.

Maybe the cops considered Zoë and me just two more urchins soiling the municipal gutters, but we had North Carolina in our future. Zoë had a Blaster, a gothic-looking mutherfucker with a Mohawk, nose stud and HOMICIDE in purple marker along the right sleeve of her jacket. We had each other to live for, so we had a heap more than any loser on the street.

Halfway into the afternoon, Zoë and I split the ramen noodles after I shook a little chicken-flavored powder onto them. Some schoolgirls came into the library and looked us over as though they'd seen us before, and they probably had. I'd dropped out because my stepdad thought I was too stupid to finish anything, and no one ever called Zoë's dad about her truancy. The girls moved along to the computers and looked at photos of boy bands and pop stars in fake lighting. Zoë pulled some Kool Aid-stained strands over her eyes and looked at me through them.

"Spoiled fucks," she said. The girls whispered to each other like girls do when they talk about boys. They chattered like stupid birds, the kind that cats always catch.

By the time the library closed, it was dark out. A plain-looking librarian with purple slacks that advertised the size of her butt lingered around the magazine rack. We twice made her say, "We're closing now," before I stood and Zoë followed my lead.

At the door, we got back into MasterBlaster mode. Zoë took her place in my armpit, and I put on my Don't Fuck With Me face. Like in a zombie movie, night was the time to be on guard. The cold was thicker than either of us could have imagined. It was a cold that lingered like sludge in the lungs.

"It's like breathing ice water," Zoë said.

Someone had made off with the tarp we'd slept under the night before, but we did find a long box as wide as a TV and lined with newspaper. It smelled sorely of Bill and the bottom was paper-thin, but we tried it anyway. I lay on top of Zoë at first, but then she complained that the gravel underneath stabbed her, so we lay on our sides with her back to me.

Even under three layers of shirt, Zoë's skin was as rigid as pig's hide. I rubbed my hand over her belly, down onto her thighs, then up over her lump-of-dough breasts and frozen nipples. I put my cheek on hers and pulled my arms around her until I could almost grab my own hips. I whispered, "I'll keep you safe, my Zozo, my Master."

Zoë took her time choosing her words. "I can't do this," she said. "I won't even last the week." Her stomach churned out one sob. "He beamed that fucking thing at my head."

This kind of cold could make anyone see nothing but the worst possible future, so I got us moving again. I was going to get us warm, dammit.

We tried rolling up in a loose drop cloth we found behind the Grace and Faith church, but it was spiky and wouldn't soften. We even tried an empty dumpster behind the very salon where that scum cunt of a girlfriend worked, but this cold was too heavy for a wind, so there was nothing to hide from. We would have frozen to the metal walls of the dumpster by morning. I dropped my three pairs of jeans and pissed on the back step of the salon, though my thighs were numb by the time I was done.

Zoë suddenly got antsy. "We'll be fucking popsicles in three days," she said. She shook her hands as though something were stuck to her fingers, as though she were looking for a barb to drive into her palm. I grabbed her hands. She pulled away, so I put my arms around her and pressed her face between my paltry tits. She wriggled and told me to fuck off and told me that she loved me and that we had to cut her dad's dick off and feed it to him and cried that we were going to fucking die.

I put my nose into Zoë's hair and smelled smoke and funk and a hint of cherry, cigarettes and Lysol and sweat and pussy. I whispered into that hair, "I got you, baby, and I'm always going to hold on to you no matter what. We're going to the Laundromat to eat Lee the Chinaman and soak in the best kind of heat."

Zoë kept squirming, so I repeated the plan, and soon she stopped smacking my sides and even bit one of my nipples tenderly. It was all the encouragement I needed to keep her safe, even if it meant splitting open my own body and letting her crawl in.

Lee the Chinaman's Takeout sat across the road from the Soap & Suds Laundromat at the edge of town near Clementon. The Ferris wheel in Clementon Park, which was closed for the season, loomed behind the Lee the Chinaman's like the negative of a magnificent sunset.

Though my Mohawk was in a serious droop under my knit cap, Lee the Chinaman still looked nervous about his health and his register with its gnarly bills that stuck up like fingers clawing their way from the grave. Zoë and I got the barbecued gizzards, the cheapest item on the Saran-wrapped menu. I had a mind to mess with the uptight Chinaman when our small, brown bag felt light, but instead I counted out his $1.19 and glared at him to make sure he didn't double-check it.

While I dribbled the remaining coins back into my pocket, Zoë said, "That's nothing to make a living on."

Zoë carried the package and the chopsticks in their red paper sleeve. Halfway across the street, she made a stabbing motion with the chopsticks.

"Asshole," she murmured. "Bastard." She twisted the chopsticks as though she were burrowing them into her dad's ear.

"I say we make a list," I said, "of who gets a broomstick hard and far up the ass."

"Who else, you mean," Zoë said.

I stroked one of her ear lobes with my thumb. "I nominate Richie," I said. My stepfather, who bought me two gifts for my seventeenth birthday: a duffel bag and an iron wrench. He kept the wrench and said he'd only show me what it was for if I ever poked my fucking ugly face through his front door again.

"The Wendy's manager," Zoë said. The one two weeks ago who gave us burgers made of spoiled meat.

I named the whole line-up of Good Charlotte for being lame-ass punks, Zoë her guidance counselor who wanted to classify her. By this time, we had crossed the parking lot and could almost feel the light from the Soap & Suds. Sometimes the owner stood just inside with a wet mop to fend off the street urchins, but tonight things were looking good for a lucky break.

Not only was the industrial-sized dryer in use, but it was also unmanned, the bench in front of it clear. The air was powdery and warm. Zoë and I stationed ourselves on that bench and watched the TV hanging over it. Two men were arguing, a woman between them. All three looked too beautiful and styled to have any real problems. I opened the carton of gizzards and used the chopsticks to stir the meat, which looked like shriveled testicles in the purple barbecue sauce.

The TV show became tedious to follow without sound, so I watched clothes fall over each other in the dryer—faded blue pajama bottoms, an occasional wool sock making an awfully high kung fu kick, some flowery pillowcases and a canvas bag, but otherwise it was wave after wave of white sheet over white sheet. Maybe the load of a night nurse. A timer counted off the minutes in red, rectangular numbers. The attendant's room was closed, the window dark. After dinner, I would help Zoë under the bench and stretch out: Blaster always took the top bunk.

Zoë ate gizzard when I offered it, but she wouldn't eat any rice. By the time the dryer finished its cycle, I had fished out every scrap of meat. I dumped the remaining rice into the sauce and shoveled up the mixture with long slurps. Zoë and I were checking out an ashtray for useable stubs when in came a woman in a puffy coat. She carried only a pink pillowcase with a damp bottom. She scanned us, nodded towards the industrial dryer to show us the cycle was done, and went to a regular dryer. Zoë's head got heavier and heavier on my shoulder, and I nudged her back awake.

"Fuck you," she said while she rubbed her forehead. "My eyelids are swelling."

"Not yet," I said. We'd been too lucky to be completely in the clear. Once it was our bright idea to sleep on benches on different sides of the room so one of us had space to bolt if a cop came in, but then I woke to find some guy stroking himself over Zoë and chanting. I got Zoë past the twisted fuck before she was too awake to notice anything.

Zoë hugged my arm. "I didn't mean it," she said. "The fuck you. I'm just tired. I love you." She squeezed my hand as though making sure I was still there.

I pulled at the black stocking peeking through a hole in Zoë's jeans. "No fuck you tonight," I said. "MasterBlaster, baby." I wanted to slide my hand down her jeans right there. And I wanted her fingers inside me in turn. I wanted to call out her name, pull on her hair and let her see my love for her.

But cold nights had no privacy. If there was heat, there was bound to be someone sharing it.

The woman in the puffy coat loaded a handful of wet cloth diapers, a bib and a boy-blue romper into her dryer. After she threw in the pillowcase, she shut the door.

"True love," she said while she patted herself for change.

Once I wanted to help Zoë open the arteries in her throat and the insides of her thighs, and then do the same for myself. We were in her room after her dad had beaten her on the shoulders with a coffee mug for knocking over a box of sugar. Zoë was stretched out on her stomach, her chin on the backs of her hands. Her breath came in sudden spasms. She stared at the door as though she expected her dad to come through and finish us both off.

I was curled into the corner, weak with the knowledge that no matter how much I threatened Zoë's dad, he made my guts curl and sent me running. All during the beating, I had done nothing more than yip like a small dog from the bedroom doorway. But I was Blaster, and I had to take action.

After finding a nail file to show her I meant business, I said to Zoë, "How about we just get out of this shit, kick back and watch from wherever we go?"

Zoë kicked at me as though I were the first wave of a gang rape. "Fuck you," she said. She sat up and pulled her jacket around her chest. "Fuck him," she said, meaning her dad. "I'm not going anywhere until I've spooned that fucker's eyes out." I knew then that Zoë only cut herself because her own arms and legs and stomach were the next best thing to hacking away at her dad. The face she made—chin out, jaw tense—was that of a boxer getting ready for a fight he would lose but never quit.

She made the same face in the Soap & Suds when Preacher Man came in.

As usual, Preacher Man had on his dingy white shirt and thin, black tie, all wrinkled. Black slacks and black shoes. An icy night, and his sleeves were rolled up to the elbows. A lit cigarette between his lips, a soft pack of Winston's in his hand. The woman with the baby clothes produced a Danielle Steele from her pocket and looked into those pages as though for an answer to some grand, unifying question that had kept her up nights.

Preacher Man fiddled with his waistband, shook the soft pack by his ear and said, "This is quite the lame party, folks."

Zoë looked at me to make sure that Blaster was good and ready to defend her, but Blaster had a jelly tumor in her gut, and she could see that.

Preacher Man limped along the row of dryers to the woman in the puffy coat. He stooped to look at the cover of the Danielle Steele and said, "Listen, kitty, when Preacher Man says he can get this party started right."

Usually, Preacher Man looking for a party was enough of a sign to move on into the night. This was clear even to the woman in the puffy coat—she pocketed her Danielle Steele and pulled open her dryer mid-cycle. The bib escaped to the floor, and she ignored it. She rushed the other items into the pillowcase.

Maybe I was still getting warm and didn't want to deal with the frigid night again. Maybe I was tired of scattering about like a timid monkey, getting pushed around by dads: Zoë's, my step dad Richie, and my real dad, who had managed to slam my face into the kitchen table on a few occasions before he clogged up enough arteries that six EMT's had to heft his load down four flights of stairs. Even when Preacher Man tried to cop a feel through the woman's puffy coat as she left, I pressed back into the bench and refused to give up my spot. If Zoë and I were outdoors for good, now was the time to take a stand. The real MasterBlaster could have breathed on Preacher Man and shriveled him into a prune.

As the woman in the puffy coat went out the door, Preacher Man said, "Bless you, kitty. Thanks for your sweet booty."

When I turned, Preacher Man was already looking our way. He smiled, and some ash jiggled off his cigarette.

"Let Preacher Man give you a smoke, buddy," he said. "You need a little cancer on this ratshit cold night." He came at us and shook his soft pack. Zoë put her face down into my chest and pulled her legs in tight.

"Just let him leer for a bit," she mumbled into my clothes. She had curled up like a beetle under attack. Her small hands took fistfuls of my shirt. "Then he'll go away."

"I got this," I told Zoë as I patted her hair. I kept my eyes on Preacher Man, who was almost to us, his soft pack extended. It was a stare down.

"Take a smoke, man," he said and said again. He looked at Zoë, then back at me, and his intentions were all too clear: Preacher Man was opening negotiations for Zoë. I could almost smell his saliva as thoughts of Zoë excited him down to his marrow. He looked over her skinny legs and the bumpy tits that I wanted to cover and hide.

I shook my head, and the realization that I was also a girl eked over Preacher Man's Halloween-mask of a face like a wash of slime. He downgraded me from pimp to just some ugly chick he had to get out of the way so he could slobber all over my girl.

"Go on," Preacher Man said as he went back to gawking at Zoë. "Preacher Man wants you to have all his smokes." He waved the pack as though it were a toy he wanted a yellow dog to chase after.

I balled up the hand closest to him and showed it. "You can still go," I said, "and keep your face in a place where you like it."

Preacher Man looked as though I had just pissed on his leg. "That's a shame to hear," he said. His eyes went from hungry to nasty as though his brain had changed channels. He was ready to tear through me with his own fingers if he had to. My lame-ass attempt at aggression fizzled and popped into darkness. Every move I had made to shake him off only let him dig in his claws a little deeper.

"Yeah, no, that's a real shame," Preacher Man said. He smiled with a predatory smugness, took the cigarette from his lips and shook ash onto his shirt. My fear must have wafted at him like bad cologne. Preacher Man was too close now to run away from with impunity. He was going to get something out of us before we could get away, and then we'd be out in the cold again in a worse position than we'd started in.

But then something unfurled inside of Zoë. She sighed and slid away from my side as though she were going to make a break for it. I didn't like the thought of running interference, but Zoë instead got to her feet, faced Preacher Man and took over.

"What you got?" she said. She was scared too, but it showed only in her eyes. Even when she stood at full height, Preacher Man had more than a foot on her. He gave her a sidelong look, as though he were trying to stare down an unpredictable gorilla.

Then Zoë did two things that both crushed me into scrap metal. First, she looked at me as though I were a full lighter that wouldn't spark. I was useless. Next, she put her hand on my shoulder, as though she were saying, "I'll take care of this." Master was putting Blaster out to pasture.

"It'll take twenty," she told Preacher Man. She leaned against my shoulder to make sure I kept my place and didn't screw up the deal, but I was nothing more now than an empty suit—limp and lacking character. I couldn't even squabble over the price. Twenty dollars promised an easier night tomorrow night, if we could stand to be with each other anymore.

Preacher Man looked Zoë over, but Zoë did nothing to entice Preacher Man any further. If Preacher Man was buying, he was getting her as-is.

Finally, Preacher Man put his hand in his pocket. "Take a walk, horse-face," was the only way he acknowledged my presence.

I wasn't moving, but Zoë held me back anyway. "It's another ten if you don't want her around," she said.

I looked away while I heard bills fold, change hands. When Zoë put the money in my hand, I had nothing left but to take it. I didn't even have enough in me to think of the names I could have been calling her: whore, slut, cunt.

"Just go outside," she said. As I left, I looked back, and Zoë was still standing in front of Preacher Man with the bench between them. Preacher Man looked subdued as he waited for her cue. Zoë wasn't going to give him his money's worth until I was out of sight, and it was probably the most loving thing she could have ever done for me.

There was a time when I knew exactly how to fix all of the tangible and intangible problems in the world. Mankind just needed to make more electricity. We all just needed to wear something blue and compliment each other regularly on our hair. As I got older, I still remembered the solutions, but the problems, once clearly defined, faded into a vague generalization that the world was fucked. Outside the Soap & Suds again, heated with a rage that was red and gangly and as sharp as piano wire, I punted a few pieces of loose asphalt, then grabbed a ratty sneaker and threw it as far as I could and screamed, "Mutherfucker!" but I didn't throw the money. That would have been too melodramatic, too stupid a thing to do. I was going to have a hard time touching Zoë again for a while as I wondered what she had given Preacher Man access to, but she wasn't going to let me leave her, and I wasn't going to stop wanting to touch her.

FIRST THANKSGIVING

Dinner had been so far civil enough, but then Patricia's father-in-law left the table without excusing himself. He furrowed his brow as though he had forgotten an important engagement—a wedding or sudden funeral.

"Melvin?" Patricia rose halfway from her seat, but Melvin was already in the front hall. The heels of his Wolverines scuffed the new linoleum. His car keys chimed, and soon he was out the door. No one else, not Melvin's wife Connie or Sam, Melvin's oldest and Patricia's husband, made a move. They studied their plates as though cautious about where their next bites should come from.

Patricia wanted to think Melvin's stage-right exit had to do with his foul mood from the ride over from Lewistown and how traffic on the Schuylkill had run like sludge. Or because the Nittany Lions had turned the ball over four times to the Wildcats in the holiday game. Or because he was less than enthusiastic about the house, a city fixer-upper in the most optimistic sense of the word. A nice neighborhood that boasted a view of the Philly skyline. When Sam gave his dad the tour, Melvin asked first who had done the handy-work before he criticized it. If the work was Sam's, Melvin approved but noted how it could have been done better. When the work was Patricia's, Melvin nodded as though it was as bad as he had expected. Indeed, Melvin rose after helping himself to Sam's stuffing with sausage and just when Connie offered him Patricia's cranberry sauce from scratch. When Melvin left the table, Connie put down the serving bowl as though she were handling radioactive isotopes.

After a few seconds of silence, Connie and Sam both came back to life. Connie brought her plate to her nose. "Mmm." She closed her eyes, a satisfied customer. "The smell alone should put me up a couple pounds," she said, and she showed, almost with pride, a smudge of lipstick on her front tooth. She was the ideal wife for Melvin: she never had anything important to say, and she never corrected him. Sam went back to shredding his turkey with his fork. Patricia tried to meet his eyes, but his gaze was too low.

And then Melvin was back, cocked and ready, with the air rifle from his truck—an RWS Model 34 single-shot, .177 caliber, 45" barrel, a light but sturdy 7.5 pounds, ammunition velocity 1,000 fps. To prevent leaks or cracks in the chamber, no air compressed until the trigger was pulled. Patricia first heard of it at the wedding reception, just six months ago. Melvin recited its write-up in *Guns & Ammo* as Canadian Club dripped from the plastic cup onto his hand.

"Now that's a weapon," he had said. "Something you don't waste on stupid shit, like bottles."

Now, without a word, he walked past the dinner table and opened the French doors to the patio. Hooch, the retriever, barked and pulled on his chain in the yard. Patricia wanted to say something, but she considered it dangerous to cross a man with a gun in his hands, even if it shot only pellets.

Sam piled up his shredded turkey and smothered it with gravy. Then he took the pepper mill and twisted it over the heap. He offered the mill to Connie, who refused it with a grin. Patricia's jaw hurt as she clenched her teeth.

Melvin squinted as he looked through the scope—the glasses he refused to wear were still packed away in Connie's pocketbook. The rifle and the buckles to the shoulder strap clicked, and a hush of breeze-blown leaves ebbed and faded before Melvin finally fired in the direction of the large oak closest to the house. The rifle reported with an acute crack, a slight hiss of air. Melvin smirked, and the deed was done. Patricia expected to hear Hooch yelp, but the man couldn't be *that* cruel, could he? Melvin leaned the rifle against the wall and closed the French doors behind him. He busied himself with something between his upper molars. The central heating kicked on, but it was going to be some time before the room got warm again.

"Hope you didn't go shooting at that darling Hooch," Connie joked as she passed Melvin the gravy boat. "He's such a good boy, Patty."

"No reason to shoot the dog," Melvin said. He poured gravy over his dark meat, potatoes and lima beans. "Dog didn't do a damn thing to anyone." Then, as if in afterthought, "With all the creatures you have out there, I'm surprised you have to feed it at all."

"Alpo's good enough for Hooch," Sam said. He laughed, and only Connie laughed with him.

Melvin mashed his food with his fork and mixed it all together. "If I were him," he said, "I'd be happier with something I killed myself."

Patricia picked up her utensils to try to make her question sound casual. "Then what did you shoot, Melvin?"

Before Melvin could answer, Sam broke in, warning Patricia out of the corner of his eye. "There's this damn tabby that hops over from next door all the time." He directed his story to Connie. "An orange and white thing. It knows Hooch is leashed-up, so the damn thing sits just out of Hooch's range, and I swear Hooch is going to pull his own head off one day." Sam laughed his fake laugh and jabbed his father in the arm. "Twenty bucks if you put a round in that puss's hindquarters."

Connie laughed.

"What did you shoot, Melvin?" Patricia asked again. Her meal was now as unappetizing as live grubs from a felled tree.

Melvin washed down his gravy mash with the cheap wine he brought, then, "The scope was all fogged up from bringing it through." He waved at the air in the dining room. "Couldn't see a thing." He took up a forkful of stuff that might have once been potatoes.

"When does the heat kick in?" he asked through a filled mouth. "I'm shriveled."

Connie sucked on her fork, Sam added more pepper, and Patricia filled her mouth with food that she couldn't swallow. The mashed potatoes liquefied and the turkey grew soft. She knew that if she spat it out she would scream and not stop.

Melvin and Connie left shortly after dinner. It was a three-hour drive back without holiday traffic. Patricia and Sam walked them out. Melvin shook Sam's hand and then held Patricia in place by the shoulders.

"That was some edible chow," he said. "You could pop me like a tick, Trish." She leaned back helplessly in his clutches. He was a regular King Kong with bad merlot on his breath. She waited for the inevitable rhyme on the nickname she'd been trying to deter him from since she first met him. Considering the occasion, she gambled on something like, "Thanks for the holiday dish."

Instead, he used her backward momentum to tilt her to the side and roll her back to him. Then he kissed her cheek. Patricia felt a sharp rub of stubble around Melvin's mouth and a cold poke from the rifle, which was slung over his shoulder.

"Next year, it's our place," Connie promised. "You'll have to come to come out to the country."

Melvin set down his rifle in the truckbed as Connie warmed the engine. "Good luck with the new house," he called out.

Sam waved. Patricia rubbed her arms for warmth and shivered.

"Be careful," she said.

Connie waved from inside the car. Melvin got in and inspected the dashboard as if expecting Connie to have loused up something already.

"He hates me," Patricia said while Sam was still waving.

"Melvin hates a long drive," Sam offered, but his voice faltered mid-lie. "He likes the house," he said afterward.

"He hates me." Patricia turned and went inside, refusing to stand there and freeze any longer. "He hates me and he hates the whole goddamn house." She didn't need to turn back to know that Sam frowned as he consider the oyster shell driveway and had nothing to say. Halfway down the block, Connie tooted the horn twice.

Patricia went to the kitchen and scooped the leftover potatoes and gravy into empty Cool Whip containers. She found slight comfort in the ping of serving spoons against china, that metallic scrape, but not all that much. Sam came in and cleared the table quietly. They had enough turkey to keep them in sandwiches for weeks. Patricia separated the light meat from the dark and wrapped each in aluminum foil. Then she stood at the sink and waited for the water to get hot.

"I'll take care of the dishes," she said to break the quiet. Sam still frowned thoughtfully while he sprayed the dishes. He was Melvin Pratt's number-one son, Sam the Man. She stoppered the drain and squeezed soap into the steaming water. While the suds built, Sam nudged her away from the sink. Patricia did not yield until he murmured, "I will." He even dared look her in the eyes.

Patricia made a production of putting on her coat, and then went out back to let Hooch run loose in the yard before bringing him in for the night. Hooch sniffed incessantly around the large oak and then dug and tore at the ground. Patricia didn't want to leave the shelter of the back doorway to get him, but when she did she found the squirrel under Hooch's paw.

It was young, barely half the size of an adult, its left paw the victim of Hooch's scratching, but the hole through its jet-black eye was not the dog's fault. The squirrel lay on its stomach as if, after falling from the tree, it tried to crawl away, then put its cheek down and gave in. There was no blood; the fur looked undisturbed and soft to the touch. Patricia came from a family of hunters. Lodge dinners with venison served in its own blood, skinned carcasses held together only by their arrays of tight, red muscles, shots echoing in the early sunlight—Patricia understood the allure of these. She liked how her dad and two brothers moved through the woods not as conquering soldiers but working stiffs with firearms. They ate what they fell. The sight of this squirrel raised something foul in Patricia's throat—a sob or bile.

She saw Sam in the kitchen window, the light on his side to prevent him from seeing anything but his own darkened reflection. He sang as he scrubbed. He danced clumsily and with little rhythm. He dropped his jaw, his mouth an exaggerated oval. Patricia thought it appropriate—Sam singing to his own reflection. Sam in a lit-up box, the Sam the Man show, hilarious but not enlightening. She held Hooch back by the collar, a weak attempt to keep at bay the natural instinct that drove him to the squirrel, and after she considered the dead animal another moment, its mouth open as if in surprise, or shock, or as though it had just tasted something ghastly, she let Hooch go back to work. Patricia looked up at the sky, where there was no moon, no stars, and she could not remember a sunny Thanksgiving. Nor could she remember rain—just clouds.

As she undressed for bed, Sam came up behind her and put his hands on her hips, his hands cold and raw from dishwater.

"Everything's clean," he whispered into her ear, his breath heavy with the rest of Melvin's wine. Patricia stepped away from him before she removed her bra and panties. She put on her nightgown quickly, her back to Sam, as though she were dressing in front of strangers. Sam started towards her again, but she hurried to bed and curled up beneath the comforter. For the first time, the mattress felt large and impersonal.

Sam sat next to her and drew her towards him with the depression he made in the mattress. He whispered in her ear, "I'm sorry," as if he wanted no one else to hear. "I'm sorry, babe." He kissed her on the ridge of cartilage just above the lobe.

"What are you sorry about?" Patricia jerked her head away from his lips. "What are *you* apologizing for?" There was a speech on the tip of her tongue, but she couldn't find any words to let it out. "Why the fuck are you apologizing?" She was tired of Sam's politic, thoughtful responses. She wanted to see him turn red and stutter and be at a loss for words. Let him blurt something out without first considering whether it was the wrong thing to say. She wanted to see his lips press white against each other. She would forgive him if he did this one thing for her.

"Let's talk about this." Sam managed a slight smile. He went to the other side of the room. He took off his pants and socks in one motion, and though Patricia used to disrobe before him with as much ease and familiarity, she could not now imagine how she had ever done so. She hugged the comforter and thought maybe she could feel warm for a moment before somehow she got to sleep. But she couldn't remember what being warm felt like, when her toes and fingers were filled with something other than chill. The fresh, never-washed smell of the comforter, which Patricia had once enjoyed as the smell of new things ahead of her, now held the odor of department store plastic.

After removing his boxers, Sam got quickly into bed and slid up behind her. She turned back and looked at him briefly, but not for long, for though he was trying to look understanding and willing to talk, he, like most men, could not help looking a little superior when naked, as though he'd made a magnanimous effort that deserved reward. Patricia could only speak to him when she looked away.

"Why did your father get out that damn gun?"

Sam grabbed her shoulder through the comforter. "It doesn't mean anything."

"He went out there and he shot a squirrel, Sam. He got up in the middle of dinner. He just got up." She blinked at her tears and tried to banish them.

Sam responded with his thoughtful silence, his willingness to look an excuse.

"He thinks he's being helpful," Sam explained, but these didn't even sound like his own words. Melvin's, maybe, or Connie's.

"You saw how much he put away." He squeezed Patricia's shoulder, but the comforter kept a barrier from her flesh. "He loved dinner tonight. And the house. If he didn't, he would have told us how much we could sell it for." He tried to massage her arm but only managed to scrunch up the stuffing. "He has his own ways of showing things, hon"—the word sounding more like a cough. "He liked the house. He wanted me to fix it up," he said, as if this made all the sense in the world.

Patricia was having a harder time holding back her tears. They had a promise between them: tell everything. A typical promise, but now she had no idea how she was ever going to live up to it. She was trying to explain things to him the best she could, but there was no telling him this, either. He pulled at the cover as though to get it away from her so he could run his raw hand over her body. If he had been any more forceful, she would have fought back. She would have kicked at him and he would have recoiled in surprise, not knowing she could have such fury in her, such indescribable passion.

"He didn't even ask," she tried. "He left the door open, too, letting all the cold air in. He didn't even tell us what he'd shot."

Sam leaned closer until his cheek was on top of his wife's head, but Patricia didn't know how she could go on with her marriage knowing a squirrel had been shot in her backyard by her father-in-law, who was responsible for Sam's nose and lips and prematurely high forehead. Sam even carried his father's name and called himself S. Melvin Pratt in grade school because he was so proud of it. Patricia was relieved she had not touched the squirrel. She did not want the smell of fur and death that now must have been stuck to Hooch's paws and nose, a smell that was impossible to both forget and live with, though Patricia knew she had to anyway.

She shivered and closed her eyes again for comfort, but then resigned to opening them again.

Sam scooted down and fit himself behind her, a thick fold of covers caught between them. He asked, "What's wrong?" and he leaned over to look into Patricia's eyes, but there was no answer he could have seen, no answer he could have understood.

Richard Weems

THEORY

Three months into my thing with Karin, she asked about my previous girlfriends. "Tell me about your prior conquests," she said, her arms and legs splayed along the length of my futon. "I have an hypothesis in development."

"Right now?" I asked from the bathroom. After disposing of the condom, I started to wash up. Karin responded, but I didn't hear her over the running water. I asked again after I turned the water off, and she said, "As good a time as any." When I came back to bed, she scootched to make room and grabbed my arm as though ready to swing over a chasm.

"*A* hypothesis," I offered by way of correction. I surrendered to her grip, my wrist at rest on a swatch of her pubic hair. "*An* apple. *An* eerie sound. *A* banana. *A* hypothesis." Karin was the one with the recent BA, but my seniority gave me the right to lecture.

Karin wiggled her lip ring with her tongue. "*An* hypothesis," she said. "If it is proper to say, 'an historical event,' logic dictates that one develops an hypothesis." An early evening screw like this, though we had reservations at a Chinese restaurant with an impressive dim sum selection, applied to Karin's Ass-Backward Theory of Dating: Karin found that men tended to be more relaxed and pleasant on a date when they'd already gotten laid and had nothing left to maneuver the evening towards.

"Would you say, 'I am going to have *an* hissy-fit,' Karin with-an-i?" I rushed through the last part as though it were a Welsh surname. I drummed my fingers on the damp, slick surface of her inner thigh as she sneered at me, Elvis-style.

Karin pulled her superior glare. "That's *an* hysterical thought," she countered. I conceded.

Karin had a host of theories about men—that men were more likely to turn women on to new music than vice versa because men depended on music to express their feelings. That the amount of space two men kept between them in a movie theatre represented their level of sexual insecurity. The subject area of Karin's current hypothesis was obvious: Though I was eleven years older than her, my apartment reeked of relentless bachelorhood. My only wall decoration was a museum print, "Flaming June," thumb-tacked above the computer. My DVD player and TV rested atop a pair of orange milk crates. With my cache of condiments, I could reconstruct barbecue beef into something resembling mango chicken. My history of relationships mimicked life expectancy before modern medicine—most died in their infancy. I could find something fatally wrong with a woman once I was determined to do so. I hadn't yet subjected Karin to this tendency since she was generally easy to be with, even though she was now digging into the roots of my romantically nomadic nature.

Karin tended coffee bar at the Hill of Beans, where I stopped en route to the sneaker shop I managed. Karin was a pleasure to watch as she poured and buttered—short, neon hair stylishly mussed, her jeans faded and torn in enticing places. One day, I came by for lunch and found her on break with a cranberry muffin. I asked her name, which was when she said, "Karin. With an i." I asked her where she got her first piercing: the standard lobe-punch, or did she start somewhere more daring? She suggested the latter, though it took some effort to find out where. I promised her a discount on some new Vans when a toxic-green toenail poked out of her present pair. She fingered the sleeve of my work shirt, which had referee's stripes, and said, "It's a date, zebra-man."

Now, "This hypothesis. About my bachelorhood, I presume?"

"You're way ahead of me, buckaroo." Karin put on a scientific expression, as though she were looking at me over the rims of glasses perched on her nose.

"Just don't try to convince me that I'm repressing a desire for men," I said.

"I've got too much evidence to the contrary." Karin slid her tongue along her lips. "So let us find the cause of this effect. Or rather say, the cause of this defect." She pulled my arm toward her body until a breast spread across my bicep. "If clothes make the man, so may his string of prior triumphs. Tell me about as many of them as you can remember. Associate freely—let one inspire you to the next. And please keep your responses to 500 words or less."

"If you're collecting data," I said, "don't you need a clipboard or something?" I swirled my fingertips against her, and Karin hogged the sheet and pulled it up to her waist. The paltry central air suddenly became quite noticeable.

"Just get rhapsodizing," she said. "I'll be the expert here."

Karin let go of my arm as I sat up and slid on a pair of gym shorts. Instead of getting dressed herself, Karin rolled to her back and picked up the book I kept next to the bed, a collection of short stories that would rock my world, according to a cashier at my store. So far, the stories were about men who behaved badly because they had nothing in their lives but shit jobs and crummy apartments or trailers. Sometimes, mean dogs dwelt under their porches. They drank and shot roman candles at cattle. They threw cans of Aqua Net into bonfires, or they plowed down corn stalks and mailboxes with their trucks. Amy, the cashier who gave me the book, got it from an English teacher who wanted to bone her. Those were Amy's words—'to bone.' One story was about a guy in his thirties banging a high schooler on her bedroom floor while her parents watched Wheel of Fortune down the hall. He kept his eye on the light from under the door. He wanted the parents to discover him on top of their little girl. He wanted that image to stay with them for the rest of their lives. Amy the cashier wore sweatpants with print across the rear—"Pink," "Aeropostale" or "What boyfriend?" Whenever I texted her about coming in to cover for a sick call, she responded with smirking emojis. When she told me how the horny English teacher talked to her cleavage, I took an involuntary peek myself, and she smiled. She had dotted the i's in the aforementioned story with tight little hearts.

And now my naked girlfriend, still pungent with the smell of our fluids, stood the same book on her breasts. She flipped some pages about and read aloud a passage about a man's guts burning with the need for recognition. Evidently, another lonely man was getting ready to spray-paint a police car or feed Alka-Seltzer to seagulls. Karin said, "Do you find your guts burning with the need for recognition? Or do you want to start telling me about your old flames now?"

I lay on my back and folded my hands over my chest as though ready to have my blood extracted with a trocar. Karin lay the book face down between her nipples and turned her face in my direction.

"Where to begin?" I said. I chose my words carefully around women, especially those I was attracted to. I could drum up a streak of witty banter easily enough, but I generally avoided unrehearsed material. Karin stared, unwilling to let me out of this testimonial.

"I made it through middle school and a year of high school without a single date," I offered as a start. "I never asked girls out because I was afraid that they would say something far more harsh than no. At my eighth grade dance, I sat by the speakers and sucked down enough half-pints of orange drink to dye my guts. High school was worse, because the other boys had PhD's in picking up girls while I was still studying for my GED, so I just pretended that I wasn't interested. When my friend Sanford's girlfriend insisted on a double-date with her friend Madge, he brought me along."

Sanford's girl turned out to be a cute Asian, Madge of course the plain-looking friend. We went to a movie together (a comedy, thoroughly unmemorable) and split off into pairs afterwards. Madge and I necked by a heating unit behind the theatre that made us laugh into each other's mouths when it snapped on and off at random. At one point, when my tongue was tired from all that flopping about, I hugged Madge and said, "I think I love you," while she bit my ear.

The next day, we talked on the phone, a two-hour conversation I didn't know I had in me. She never brought up my awkward profession of love, but I could already feel it weighting the air between us. A week later, we met at the same theatre for another date. My plan was a repeat performance—movie, then another smooch-fest by the heating unit. But this movie had a scene where an old woman snuck through a bedroom window and fell onto a couple having acrobatic sex under the covers. The little old woman wobbled around on top of them as though on a sand dune in the middle of an earthquake.

I slid the book off Karin's chest. "I can say now that the sex was unrealistic," I said, "all that reeling and moaning and legs flailing, but I had no idea at the time that people did it any other way." I could still remember the way Madge held my hand and stared at the screen with a slight grin.

Karin said, "So the roly-poly sex bothered you?"

"It wasn't the roly-poly so much," I said. Madge had me hungry for some necking, but that exorbitant fucking up on the screen made me nervous. Could Madge have picked this movie because she wanted to have sex with me? I had no idea how we were going to roll around like that behind a theatre and finish up before my mom came to get me. "Does that make any sense?"

Karin looked as though mine were a rhetorical question. "How did she taste?" she said after another long pause.

"When?"

"That first kiss. How did she taste?"

"That was an entire date ago. Have I spoken for naught about witnessing an accidental ménage a trois while sitting next to my very first girl?"

"One question at a time," Karin said. "This is scientific, after all. I just need to follow up on some possibly revealing information. What did this Madge taste like?"

"I don't know," I said. "Metallic. I didn't like how she tasted, but it was my first kiss and I knew I had to get used to the flavor if I ever wanted to make out again."

Karin took Amy's book back and flipped through it as though she were looking for an answer key. "And during date the second, you weren't sure how you were going to manage some nookie with this Madge and keep to your curfew?"

"This Madge," I said. "Are you expecting others?"

"If you like, we can call all of your old girlfriends Madge. This one can be Madge$_1$, if you want to preserve some anonymity." Karin smirked, but had I decided to revise all the names on my romantic credit history, she would have gone along. People told Karin intimate details about themselves because she carried an air of humble omniscience —she never looked surprised or shocked at any revelation. Her boss at the Hill of Beans revealed to her that he embezzled a hundred pounds of coffee beans a month and sold them on eBay. The pale, flat barista with a purple streak in her jet black hair fantasized about being a gay boy and had once paid five hundred dollars for a seminar on anal masturbation. Karin's roommate, Devin, a thoroughly unwashed guy who had long ago given his life up to watching television, was a secret fan of Hanson, a briefly popular teeny-bopper band of blond brothers, and had a slew of fan blogs and interviews from teen-beat magazines bookmarked in his browser.

"There was only one Madge," I said, "but I'm not sure that I'm always going to be able to give names." For some, I remembered only what turned them on the most, whether they preferred to sit on my left or right, how they were lousy kissers or didn't know what to do with their hands. Some threatened to have major breakdowns if I didn't call them again, so of course I didn't. Bland, scared women who worried aloud about their attractiveness and asked for progress reports mid-date, women who handed out roadmaps to their insufficiencies and the shortcuts to breaking their hearts. For some, I remembered their kids more easily than I remembered them. But what could Karin learn from all of these lost causes?

"There are just a lot of them," I said. "It's going to be hard to sort some of them out."

"Then we'd better finish up with your first girl so we can get moving," Karin said. "You're way over your word limit, but I'll consider this a warm-up."

The evening was temperate enough to keep the heating unit quiet, but Madge and I still broke out laughing every now and then because there was nothing else to interrupt neck session #2. Even worse, she said nothing about the boff-fest we had just witnessed onscreen, so I had to guess whether she was looking to get it on out here, or if she was planning our life together now that I loved her, even though I had only ever kissed or held hands with this one girl. I dared to bring my hand down low enough to finger a loop in Madge's waistband. She hummed into my mouth, a hum that could have been a warning as much as encouragement, so I backed off. Then she brushed up against my erection and put her hand on it. I snapped back as though she had aimed a fist at my balls.

"She had clearly made out with boys before," I said. "If she was a virgin, it was only by technicality. I was in far too unfamiliar territory to risk taking the plunge."

"So you sucked out each other's esophagi until your mom picked you up," Karin said. "Did you ever get comfortable with a Madge crotch-grab?"

I didn't. Just two days after the second date, I wrote her a Dear Madge email. "The embarrassment," I explained to Karin, "was that I had told her that I loved her on the first date, but of course I gave every reason I could think of except that one." In the letter, I predicted that she would consider my email a chicken-shit way of breaking up with her, and I told her I wouldn't call her again. I wrote other things too, about four pages' worth, but I couldn't remember any of it now.

"Damage done," Karin said.

"And so ends the saga of Madge." I put out my hand as though signaling for applause to the orange-decked woman in the Leighton print push-pinned to the wall. That, or the first volley of eggs. "So does this explain why I'm a little shit who avoids commitment?"

But instead of taking the bait for a compliment, some assurance that I wasn't so bad, Karin stared at the ceiling as though she were ordering bubbles of information up there. "One example does not a pattern make," she said. "Especially when it comes to starter-relationships. How often do you tell girlfriends that you love them?"

"There was one other," I said, but I wasn't ready to talk about her yet. "She didn't come right after Madge, though. This was much later." After Madge, I learned how to talk to girls, how to get them to want what I wanted from the start. Before Karin, I was wondering if I had the stuff of long-term commitment in me, or if I was the type who would end up buying a wife from Guam.

"Men," Karin said, and she snapped shut Amy's book as though she meant all of us, living and literary alike. "I don't need chronological narrative. Hell, I don't need narrative. Let's do it this way." She sat up and put her hand on my chest. "This is very important. Think in blurbs. The key here is not so much covering the whole story with adequate closure, but honing each relationship down to the details you find most important or memorable, as well as how you move from one to the other, what inspires you to your next item. Keep moving. Keep a broad perspective. Don't burden me with all the snitty particulars."

I cupped one of her breasts to let her know where I expected this interview to go. She didn't respond to my touch, but she didn't ward me off, either.

"All right, then," I said. "Do you mean something like, 'I dated a marathon runner who talked only about what she didn't want in a relationship'?"

She leaned forward and kissed me. It was a wet kiss, a reward. "You got it now, bub. Short and to the point."

"The runner," I said. "She had amassed a litany of details she didn't like about her past boyfriends and thought reviewing this shopping list on the first date would make all of her future relationships start off on the right foot. She didn't think watching porn was sexy, nor did she want a boyfriend to ever refer to her butt in public. She told me how much she hated it when a guy pushed her head down into his lap. We dated for two months. She used her hand on me, and we dry-humped a couple of times, but she freaked out when she realized she wanted to go all the way with me. That was supposed to explain why she didn't want to see me again. How about that?"

"Not bad," Karin said. "Was this still in high school?"

"This was two girlfriends ago," I said. "She worried about how I was going to describe her after we'd broken up. She brought this up on our second date. She said, 'I'm going to sound so awful when you say, "You won't believe this one girl I used to date."'"

"That's funny," Karin said. "You said that she said what you were going to say. You must be disappointed to realize she had reason to worry." Karin gave me another wet kiss, this time a little longer, and she put my hand on her ass. "Now you're getting the hang of it." Karin had a calm, reassuring tone that could have talked down a jumper. "Keep them coming. Who does the neurotic hand-job runner bring to mind?"

I told Karin about an older woman who dated me because I reminded her of a boyfriend she regretted breaking up with. This mytho-historical ex had taken her to premieres and galleries in Greenwich Village, but she couldn't attend such things anymore because she didn't want to bump into him, so before me she dated rednecks who fucked around on her.

"She wanted to be with someone who had at least read a book or two, could watch a movie and understand the plot, even when there wasn't much of one." When we had sex, she refused to look at me. I found out later that she was still doinking some married rig-driver.

Then I told Karin about a divorcee who couldn't bring herself to have sex with other men yet. Our dates would end on a rather lukewarm note, with some kissing until she couldn't go any further, but as soon as I got home she would call and ask me if she should spank herself. I'd tell her yes, she should. Then she'd tell me how she was pulling down her panties and bending over the arm of the sofa, and I'd tell her to smack herself harder, harder. She'd ask me if I was playing with myself. I always told her yes, even if I wasn't, and she'd tell me how one day we would do this in person. One night, after dropping her home, I went to a local bar and took home a sagging, lonely woman who let me do all the things I was only allowed to imagine with the divorcee. The divorcee's messages piled up, and I erased them. Every now and then, usually after some drinking, I would call and maybe get things started over the phone again, but then I would avoid her for months again.

I paused. "What a story to tell the woman you're sleeping with, eh?" I said.

Karin played with the ties on my gym shorts. "Don't think," she said. "You'll throw off your momentum. I'll make the conclusions here, if you don't mind."

Karin had lured me into stark, raving honesty. Details came to mind, and I handed them over without a moment's editing. Karin listened to them without a hint of disgust or disappointment. I wanted to hear Karin's conclusion for my regular bouts of loneliness, my spans between girlfriends that, whether momentary or prolonged, made me wonder why I couldn't find any sane women in the world.

So I told Karin about the woman I once proposed to. I had no particular reason for wanting to get married—maybe because she was from Alabama and had an accent as smooth as yogurt. Maybe because I was still in college and hadn't yet grown tired of working long hours only to write checks to pay off my tuition bills. Maybe because everyone else thought her name was Lindsay, but that she had confided to me that her name was Linseed, as in the oil. Linseed and I were hanging out in someone's dorm room, and I dared her to go to City Hall with me. She thanked me with all her powers of Southern charm, though I insisted I was serious. Because she turned me down, I cheated on her the very next weekend at another party. In plain sight, I made out with a redhead who had dared me to guess what color underwear she was wearing. I grabbed at the redhead while Linseed, the woman I had proposed to a kegger ago, yelled, "That's my man," to no avail.

I stopped as though someone had just given me a well deserved shake. I had always considered myself the scorned lover seeking comfort, Linseed aware of her mistake only too late. This was the version I had convinced myself was the most accurate, but with Karin the word "cheat" slipped out of me as easily as if it had been dipped in a slick coating of truth.

"So I'm a cheater," I said in summation. "I cheated on the woman I proposed to."

Karin leaned over my chest and glowered. "What did I tell you about making conclusions? We're looking for patterns here, correlations that lead to causality. You can't be a cheater if you only did it once."

Karin's statement was like a challenge to my honor, so I had to prove to her that I was, in fact, a cheater. Thus, I told her about cheating on a girlfriend I had just moved in with, the only other woman to whom I had said, "I love you," even after having cheated on her. Two days after we moved her stuff into my place, I met up with Ellen, an old friend from high school, and Ellen and I made out in front of a pizzeria across the street from my sneaker shop. She was in a relationship too, a guy she would end up marrying. Ellen and I agreed to keep that night a secret, and I went home to my freshly moved-in girlfriend. I made vague overtures about how boring it was to meet up with high school friends and continued living with her for eight months until she realized I had no intention of marrying her.

"I'm still not sure how it happened," I said to Karin. "Ellen wasn't an old girlfriend. I knew her through a friend of mine, a guy she dated my senior year, when a bunch of us would drink in the woods together. Ellen and I ate pizza and talked about old times. Then we hugged out front and started kissing."

"Funny how stuff like that just happens," Karin said. She rested her cheek by my right nipple. How could someone look so dispassionate while her boyfriend told her about his adventures in philandering? I wanted her to be angry with me, or at least proud that I could be so forthcoming. I wanted some sign that what I was saying was revelatory. I was tempted to tell Karin about a fantasy of mine: I walk into the back room of the sneaker shop while Amy is stocking shelves, and we have sex on one of those shitty folding chairs —quiet, quick and painless—with the other clerks and customers talking size and width and pricing on the other side of the flimsy black curtain. Then we go back to work as though nothing happened. We still flirt with each other, make suggestive remarks—every now and then I bend her over in the back room—but everything else in my life remains exactly as it was before I started boning my seventeen year-old clerk.

But I kept this to myself. Karin leaned her elbows into my chest and propped up her chin with her hands. "And did you have sex with your high school friend that night?"

"No," I said, and I was embarrassed to admit it. I tried —I told Ellen that this was our one and only shot, and shouldn't we go ahead and go somewhere together (motel room, car seat)? But Ellen only pushed my hands away when I ran them down her back or reached for her breasts. We made out for an hour or so. She told me how much she loved me, and I told her that maybe we could reunite some other time. My live-in girlfriend texted me eight times during the whole incident, each one adding to the number of question marks in the previous.

Karin shook her head and ground her elbows alternately into my ribs. She even chuckled.

"I'm glad you're amused," I said.

She smiled, as though she had a follow-up that would put everything in perspective. "You haven't told me anything about the girlfriend you lived with," she said. "Except for cheating on her, of course."

That was when I understood: I had lost Karin. She had come over tonight not for dim sum, but to say goodbye—but not before she seduced me into explaining for her all the reasons she needed to leave me.

"I came home and had sex with my live-in girlfriend," I said, my voice quiet and strained. I took Karin's hand and spoke as though fessing up to some great, unsolved crime I couldn't bear living with anymore. "Leigh. Her name was Leigh, and I turned her around so I didn't have to look at her face. I came and I came, and every time it was for Ellen. I had sex with the girlfriend that I was in love with, but I was really having sex with another woman, and it was probably the best sex ever, because I was having sex with both of them." All of this rolled out of me as though telling Karin every ounce of truth I could muster would somehow negate it all and prove I was no longer that kind of person. I even told Karin about how I fantasized about Amy, and Karin scrunched up her face as though annoyed I had repeated myself.

"And how did it end with the woman you lived with?" Karin said as though she had led me through a lesson we were now wrapping up. Like a good teacher, she was letting me connect the dots myself. As I talked, I swear she moved her lips along with my words as though she already knew everything that was going to come out of my mouth.

"She moved out," I said. "She said living separately would bring us closer, but as soon as she had her own place, she came over and said I was a wonderful man. She kissed me and said she loved me and sat on my lap. She kissed me with her eyes open." This was in the very living room down the hall from my bed. After two months of staring at blank walls, I bought the print of "Flaming June" and tacked it up, as though the woman in the print could offer any kind of company. "She never once said that it was over, but I cried anyway."

"You cried?" Karin squinted with doubt.

"You're right," I said. "I was upset, but I didn't cry. I just felt lonely. Again."

"You never had sex with two women." Karin crept out from under the sheet. "You didn't have sex with either of them, and that was what made it the best sex ever...for you."

I still haven't figured out that sentiment. Karin had, by this time, climbed on top of me. She took my hands and placed one on her breast, the other on her hip. She reached back to ease down my gym shorts.

"One more time," she said. Out of loneliness, I made every move she wanted me to.

JOHN & XENIA

On Friday, John put together a special dinner for the two of them—mee grob, pad thai, and two orders of something he called 'the red stuff.' The manager of the Bangkok Palace always smiled when he took John's order and was kind enough not to correct him. At his apartment, John lit apple-scented candles, put red bulbs in the dining room chandelier and arranged a tray of Ho-Ho's and Cool Whip for dessert. When Xenia came through the door, she put one fist on her hip and glared at him.

"You're either getting back with your wife," she said, "or you've accepted a teaching gig in Mongolia."

John scooped up a pile of the red stuff with his chopsticks. "Looks purple in this light, doesn't it?"

Xenia sneered and brandished her fingernails. "I have glue all over my hands," she said, "and I'm not afraid to use it." Xenia made postcards that sold at bookstores and coffee shops. She stepped out of her sneakers and walked to the table while picking intricately at her fingers.

When she sat down and picked up the bowl of pad thai, John said, "We've been together six months."

Xenia put her lips to the edge of the bowl. "Horse puckey," she said, and she shoveled a wad of noodles into her mouth. Then, while chewing, "You're way off, stud. It was two years ago, when I was Minnie Mouse."

"You're full of shit," John said, as he pushed out his lower jaw to keep mee grob in his mouth. John had never told Xenia about his one trip to Disney World, but he kept a picture from it by his bed. The picture was of him and his son, Calvin, standing before the photogenic castle. Calvin was five, and it was their first week together after the separation. The boy looked like he was studying something on the camera lens.

But until this moment, John had forgotten about the Minnie Mouse thing. Late into their third day at the Magic Kingdom, Calvin was walking like Dopey on anti-psychotics. Then it was announced that Mickey, Minnie, Donald, Chip and of course Dale were making an appearance in the gift shop. Calvin grabbed his father's hand and said, "Gift shop." The lines were equally long for each character, but Calvin insisted on meeting Minnie. He grinned like a Labrador when she patted his head delicately with her oversized white glove.

"When were you ever Minnie Mouse?" John said. Xenia had told him a lot of stories about her past, and he felt it was his duty to refute them. According to her, she'd been a crop duster in Des Moines, a champion Indian wrestler with a traveling carnival, as well as the first dancer/bouncer at Chi-Chi's Gentleman's Club in San Francisco. She had the leg strength to lend credence to the wrestler story, but John had a hard time accepting that anyone could live such an interesting life and be much younger than him. "Should I tell you now how cute your butt looked in that polka-dot dress?"

Xenia sucked up a clump of pad thai and glared at him over the rim of the bowl. "It was two months," she said, "before I could meet the populous in that poorly ventilated mask." She went on: Disney had regulations for playing their characters, like not crossing the plane of the eyebrows when patting a child's head. There was no talking, either—even a sticky-faced four year-old could sniff out a bad Minnie Mouse imitation. But most of all, cardinal rule uno (she thrust out a forefinger to emphasize this), she was never, *ever* to remove her mask in public, even if nauseous or on the verge of fainting. "Get sick in your head, they said, and make sure it doesn't dribble out, because those uniforms are expensive."

It was one of her better stories—sensible, streamlined and not weighed down with frivolous detail. But John couldn't rebut her with the tale of their first meeting because he couldn't remember it. Somewhere into a string of dingy bars and lonely women, he must have met Xenia and forgotten her just as quickly, because at a dive called The Golden Well, as he waited for his up at a pool table, Xenia punched him in the arm and said, "A red sawbuck says you don't remember my name." Fifteen years his junior, with dark, Greek features that looked almost pale next to her ink-black hair, she was far better than the divorced, almost-forty English teacher had any hope of scoring with. Within a month, Xenia had given him the key to her apartment (in truth a motel room) and introduced him to her neighbors, a colony of retirees who seemed surprised that Xenia knew their names.

John offered Xenia the red stuff, but she was deep into the mee grob. He considered a fried shrimp between his chopsticks as he said, "I don't think I could train that long to be someone else's character."

"I quit the day I met you, bub." Xenia spat a noodle fragment at him and ran her stockinged feet up John's calves. All the nerves in Xenia's body must have connected at the feet—she preferred touching him this way. "Took me eighteen months to figure out you lived in Jersey."

"You looked for me?" John's smile was full of doubt, but the idea intrigued him all the same.

"A noodle dinner," she said, "under red light. Five will get you one there are Hostess cakes for dessert." Xenia aimed her round, green eyes directly into his. "You realize this is getting serious, don't you?"

The next night, Xenia offered to cook. That meant pork chops seared in an overheated pan with no oil. John usually did his best to decline her dinner invitations, but she said it was her turn to do something special for him, so he came over and ate with little comment.

Xenia was quiet during most of the meal, then while John was cutting meat from the bone asked, "So what's your ex's name?"

John put down his knife and fork because he thought it would make him look serious when he said, "I'm not comfortable talking about that with you yet."

John usually liked Xenia's smile, especially the moment before it happened, when her lips tensed as though her teeth had suddenly inflated and couldn't be hidden anymore. He didn't think this was a moment that called for one of her smiles, but he never understood her sense of humor. She smiled, then laughed, then said, "Yet you can tell me about your boy, who carries the namesake of an unmemorable president. She must have dropped you like blood pressure."

John had little problem when Xenia teased him or did little things to frustrate him. It was like dealing with one of his students, in a way. But this was a subject he saw nothing worth making a joke out of.

"Is she bigger than a bread box?" Xenia asked, but John kept his eyes from her. He maintained his angry posture even when she took his hand, but he could feel his will crumbling as she whispered in his ear.

"I can name that ex in one letter," she said.

It was going to be a long, tense night if he didn't cave a little: Xenia never lost a battle of wills.

"Dawn," he said.

Xenia leaned in close to his face. "As in Tony Orlando and?"

Damn her. John couldn't help but smile, but he refused to laugh. Xenia sang, "Oh dear Papa, please pray for me."

"That's not even them!" Now it was a laugh. Xenia was still holding his hand.

They finished dinner and went out dancing. Because they could never agree on music they both liked, they went somewhere they both hated, a golden oldies club with a DJ who talked constantly over the music. Xenia had an art for moving rhythmically, while most of John's efforts went to keeping his arms and feet coordinated. After a string of songs named after dances neither of them knew, they went to his place.

John rushed to the bathroom as soon as they got through the door and left his phone by the door. When he came out, he heard Dawn's usual pre-visitation message in the living room:

"...can't have milk this weekend because he has a bit of a cold." She sounded like a history professor reading from yellowed lecture notes. Xenia was seated on the floor with John's phone in her lap. "He needs new sneakers for basketball, and he needs to be home two hours early Sunday, so I will meet you at three instead of five. Again, that's three o'clock p.m. instead of five." For this last sentence, Dawn enunciated each syllable completely.

"That's the thing about back-up singers," Xenia said. She pulled her knees to her chin and let the phone drop. "They just don't speak like us normal folk." Fortunately, it was the last John heard of his ex-wife for the rest of the night.

And after only a few hours of sleep, Xenia prodded him awake.

"Time to make the donuts." She poked him in the ribs and upper abdomen. She licked her finger and stuck it in his ear.

John sat up with a humph, but there was nothing he could say when he saw Xenia in the light of a brightening sky, half her face and one breast an exquisite shade of purple.

Xenia crawled forward on the bed and shoved John towards the bedroom door. "Make the goddamn donuts."

John got up and showered. While running water on the back of his neck, he murmured, "Frigging donuts," down into his chest hair. After drying off, he went to the kitchen to make coffee.

And for just a moment before swinging open the door he was sure that behind it would be tall, multi-shelved ovens and rolling carts with trays full of strawberry-frosted, jelly and chocolate honey-glazed. The image was so vivid that the sight of his empty table and the single plate and glass in the dish rack made him wonder if he was in the wrong apartment. The feeling faded quickly, but not without leaving a metallic taste of nostalgia for a childhood John never had: young days spent in the warm and sweet air of a bakery, the kitchen floor so thick with flour it was like walking on baked crust.

Taped to the coffeemaker was a note from Xenia: "It's settled. You and me and the former president have a date. See you by the bumper cars." John took the note from the coffee maker and stuck it to his mug. Perhaps it was time after all.

During his drive north, John practiced aloud introductions between Xenia and his son, but no matter how innocuously he put it, he knew the ends would be the same. Calvin was going to tell Dawn that Dad had a girlfriend. That meant an interrogation from Dawn. Dawn believed that if something couldn't be explained objectively, it didn't really exist. But what could he have told her that explained objectively what he liked about Xenia? That Xenia called seagulls 'monkeys' because of the similarity in their voices? That pizza trays in cafeterias, the way they revolved until the door opened, mesmerized her? That she spoke French in her sleep?

John was clenching his jaw, had been doing so for several mileposts. Thoughts of his seven-year marriage produced lumps of shame behind his clavicle. The way Dawn maneuvered for months towards their separation, so that when she did announce it, there was barely anything he could have called their communal property anymore. She even presented him with a preliminary visitation schedule. All she wanted from him was agreement. And he gave it

The meeting spot was in the Cheesequake Rest Area, in front of a Burger King. Though John's drive was longer,

Dawn was always late by the same degree. He sat on the rail, cars speeding behind his back, and looked at nothing in particular until Dawn showed up.

Dawn drove at attention. Calvin was in the back, using his weekend bag as a pillow. John opened the passenger door of his car to speed up the exchange.

"You got my message?" Dawn said. Before getting an answer, she reached back and kneaded Calvin's bare knee a couple times. "Got to switch over now, honey." Her red hair was professionally windblown. She was wearing a sleeveless top, her arms pale and taut like torsion cable. Whenever she showed her arms like that, John wanted to squeeze her shoulders.

Calvin transferred to John's car with barely a hint of opening his eyes. While the boy was buckling himself in, John went over to Dawn's window. He leaned on the door and said, "You should keep your hair short like that."

"It's easier to keep up," Dawn said. She was looking past him at Calvin. "He's got a bit of a cold."

"I got the message," John said. He hoped she wouldn't take it as him being snide, but she was always a tough read.

Dawn kept her eyes off him. "He'll probably sleep the whole way down."

"I'll keep the radio low, then."

They were quiet a moment, Dawn's Jetta running smoothly, then she said, "How are you?" as though she couldn't think of anything else to say.

"Nothing to report," he said, though she'd without doubt take that one as snide. She nodded and raised her window. He waved to her as she left, but because of her sunglasses he couldn't tell if she saw him or not.

Calvin slept soundly all the way to John's apartment. John left him in the car while he took Calvin's bag in. When he was pulling back out, Calvin sat up and rubbed his face.

"Where now?"

"We're going to meet a friend of your dad's."

Through the rearview, John watched Calvin stare out the window next to him. The boy clearly had questions, but he was still trying to form them. John and Dawn had always kept their dealings civil for Calvin's sake, but for moments like these maybe a little yelling and carrying on may have done Calvin some good—viewed from the side, Calvin was as stoic as Jefferson on the nickel.

"You'll like this friend of mine," John said. "Those elephant jokes your mom tells? Xenia's got a ton of them." He hoped his son would look at Xenia as another kid, only bigger.

At the amusement park, Xenia waited for them by a trashcan shaped like a hippopotamus. She had on a luau shirt and baggy shorts, her bob slicked flat against her skull.

"Are you my dad's girlfriend?" Calvin asked as he shook Xenia's hand. John fought the urge to pull the boy back and review with him what 'friend' meant. He also made a note to himself—ask Calvin if that handshake felt at all familiar.

Xenia changed her and Calvin's grip so they looked ready to arm-wrestle. "I get to ride the bumper cars for free whenever I want," she said, "and I get to ride as long as I feel like it. That's because I'm the best of all time. You taking me on?"

Calvin nodded as though he were having a bad reaction to some medication. The two of them raced up the ramp and got in line. When it was their turn, Xenia declared to the attendant, "I am the dowager-empress of these here bumper cars. I demand the two best carriages, and we will not relinquish them until we are full well bumped out, capisce?"

Calvin took his cue from Xenia squeezing the top of his head. "The green one."

Xenia said, "We will tell you when we are finished, dear peasant." When Calvin had taken off for his chosen vehicle, she handed over a healthy stack of tickets.

As Xenia and Calvin waited for their first round to start, Calvin waved to his dad. Xenia waved too. John took a seat by the exit ramp and declined all offers to join them.

Xenia and Calvin rode the bumper cars for close to an hour, then they all went for pork roll and birch beer. Xenia bet Calvin a million and six dollars that she could hum "The Song That Doesn't End" the longest. Though the contest made John's brain threaten to shoot straight from his skull, especially when they were all in his car going back to his place, Calvin looked goofier and more child-like than he had in two years of weekend visits. Thankfully, Xenia and the boy played a revised form of Uno in the bedroom while John did some grading in the kitchen. The bet must have been somehow settled or forgotten, because after a while, Calvin called out, "Red." A bit later, the boy yelled, "Baked." Xenia responded with, "Garbanzo, otherwise known as the chickpea." John was curious to see what kind of play required the calling out of different types of bean, but he didn't want to get hooked into the game. He had too much work to do.

For dinner, Xenia made a motion for macaroni and cheese, and Calvin seconded. While eating, the two of them laid noodles out on their napkins and traded them like baseball cards. Xenia bargained hard for macaronis with tight arcs. But as soon as she was finished eating, she stood, addressed Calvin as "Mister President, retired," and saluted him. When Calvin saluted back, she put her dishes in the sink and promptly left. John tried to prepare some explanation as to why Xenia was gone, but Calvin just kept eating, his gaze focused as though humming to himself. After dinner, and after Calvin finished his math homework, father and son watched a Power Rangers movie. At one point, Calvin said, "I'd be the green Ranger."

John considered the matter seriously before answering. He liked the Red Ranger, the charismatic leader, but knew in the end that he had to answer realistically. "I think I'd be the blue one." He was the more technical one, brainy, a little less inclined to pick a fight.

Calvin put his head back on the cushion. "And Xenia?"

John shook his head. "I don't know, buddy." He had no clue what kind of absurd color she'd invent for herself.

Sunday went along with much of the usual routine—Calvin watched television, alternating between the Weather Channel and Nickelodeon, while John got things ready for his next week of classes. But just minutes before they were to leave, the boy called his mother. John didn't eavesdrop, though he wanted to. Nor did he ask Calvin during the drive north what he said to Dawn about Xenia.

They had to wait, as usual. Calvin stood on the guardrail and watched cars speed by. John watched how the boy mouthed silently each car's make.

For the exchange to give Calvin back, John didn't have to wait alone. The Burger King parking lot was a popular site for fathers giving back their children. Sometimes there was yelling, or voices raised to the point of yelling, but the Row of Woe, as John liked to think of it, was for the most part a trading post of quiet transactions, the details settled previously through repetition and text conferencing. Every now and then, one father stole a few deep kisses with his ex in the front seat of her BMW while their fraternal twins went out for burger value meals.

Dawn pulled in and got out of her car, which was usually a sign that she had something to say, some reminder of what John had done wrong. She was wearing a bright green sundress, her arms bare again. First, she looked over to Calvin and called out, "Hi, honey." Then she looked at John.

"What's she like?"

John gave her the first thing that came to mind. "She's a lot of fun," he said.

"Calvin said the same thing."

"The boy has taste."

Dawn had a "You know what I mean" look, but John didn't know what she was asking. Still, she kept staring at him. It was a moment John wanted Calvin to dispel, especially since he felt he was on the verge of apologizing for having a girlfriend. He turned to the boy and called out, "Mr. President."

Calvin responded immediately and left his survey of the traffic. Dawn shook her head slightly.

While Calvin got into his mother's car, Dawn said to John, "Are you happy with her?"

John wanted to say he was happy with Xenia, but what kind of happiness that was seemed just beyond his range of understanding, like a perfect word that would put everything in perspective…if he could just remember what that word was.

"I don't think I have an easy answer for that," he said.

Dawn looked off towards the Burger King. "You shouldn't."

John waved as Dawn pulled away. He rubbed his neck and face and thought about how nice it was to know Xenia was going to be in his apartment when he got home, and that she was going to tug his sleeve and bug him for dinner.

Yet there was also a voice, maybe one of those smug, self-assured voices that's especially annoying because it really is, in fact, always right. Maybe the voice of his better nature, or Dawn's voice. It passed through him too quickly to identify who it was.

The voice told him that Xenia was going to break his heart.

One way Xenia produced postcards was to get old photographs from antique & collectibles stores and make collages out of them: Oscar Wilde leaning on the Mona Lisa's shoulder; ladies with Trotsky heads on the ends of parasol sticks; anguished woman with a giant pear in her lap. When she had a dozen of them ready, she'd put them face down in a pile and write a caption on the back of each without looking to see what collage it was. The results would be something like this:

For Oscar and Mona, "I think the Buddha had something to say on that subject."

For the ladies toting beheaded Trotsky's, "The flowers are nice this time of year."

The pear woman sighed into a balloon floating above her crooked arm, "I so love Austen."

Xenia also made postcards from unusual pictures she'd take on sudden road trips. She disappeared for four days straight once, and her only explanation to John when she returned was, "Work."

This time, it was the weekend Xenia had promised Calvin a special dish of macaroni and cheese: Flintstone noodles mixed with Animaniacs ("Stoned-a-maniac-and-cheese," she called it).

She woke John by biting his nose. She was dressed in purple leotards and his white shirt. She had a camera around her neck, and she put a five-dollar bill in his mouth.

"This is for 3-Walled Night," she explained. "Get the baby some tuna. Lock up. Finish the milk or throw it out."

3-Walled Night was not her cat. Its real name was Dusty, but Xenia would take him in for days at a time and read to him from Samuel Richardson's *Clarissa*. Her theory was that if a cat read to from the longest novel in the English language would learn to talk, though probably with an English accent.

"My shirt," John grumbled, trying to spit the money from his dry lips.

"It's warm," Xenia said. "You won't need it."

John was still trying to get his bearings. "What about Calvin's lunch?"

"I'll send stuff," Xenia said. She bit his nose again, this time with affection. Then she was off the bed and soon out the door. As she left, she snapped the waistband of her tights against her belly and hummed Tchaikovsky.

The weekend passed quietly: no word from Xenia at all. Calvin went back to his old sobriety and didn't ask about her once. He ate nothing but grilled cheese all weekend. He must have said something to Dawn on the phone, because at the exchange she stepped up close to him and said, "Are you two still seeing each other?"

John hadn't been this close to her in a long time. She smelled of strawberry shampoo and hand lotion. Somehow, it made him not want to squeeze her shoulders anymore.

"She had somewhere to be," he said.

Monday, John started getting postcards. Actually, they were advertisements disguised as postcards that could be picked up for free at restaurants and bars. These were the only postcards Xenia either disliked or respected enough to write on.

She had gone south. Maryland, Virginia, Kentucky, back into Virginia, then straight into South Carolina. That, or the post offices in some areas weren't regularly picking up the mail. She didn't sign any of them, but who else would have sent a postcard with "Whoppers are by far the pet rock of the new millennium" scrawled almost illegibly by John's address? If advertisement copy filled up the verso side, she highlighted parts to make new ideas. "Tabletop radios are popular for their convenience and small size" became "able pop for the con mall."

She returned late Friday evening, refusing to apologize, and when John tried to explain how confused he was over when she'd be back, if she'd be back at all, and how disappointed Calvin was, she played the world's smallest violin with her thumb and middle finger. He gave her the postcards she'd sent, to show her he'd saved them and that they meant something to him, but she only flipped through them as though looking for animated sequences. Then she handed the stack back to him and said, "Vile. If I had gotten crap like this in my mailbox, I'd've shredded them immediately."

There was little more to say after that. It was obvious she was out to do everything she could to irritate him. He hadn't seen a face like that, rebellious and obstinate, since Calvin was three.

"I'm glad all this matters to you so much," John said.

And Xenia laughed. Her eyes turned manic and her laughing was forced, but effective just the same. He left her like that in the living room, and he slammed the bedroom door and yelled, "Dammit," until he no longer felt like knocking over the nightstand. Xenia continued to laugh. John forced himself to keep quiet, then he heard her leave. Later, after knowing he'd not be able to sleep, he found that she'd exchanged the cushions between his couch and loveseat. She'd also switched bulbs between the standard lamp and the 3-way, but the postcards had vanished altogether.

The next night, there was a party thrown by one the teachers at John's school. John shaved and put on a tie, and when he went outside he found Xenia sitting on the hood of his Toyota. She was in a black T-shirt, black tights and a purple skirt—her version of formal wear. She was tearing pages from a book on interior design and storing them under her thigh.

"I've got to go," he said.

She didn't look up from the book. "Fashionable tardiness can do wonders for the soul."

John stood there, fingering his keys. Finally, Xenia said, "Yes, you do have to go." She picked up the torn pages and hopped off his car. With her free hand, she traced the pattern in his tie, then said, "Other teachers will be there, yes?"

John nodded but said nothing.

Xenia held the end of his tie to her mouth and kissed it. "For luck," she said. She pulled an envelope from the waistband of her skirt and pressed it to his chest.

"Also for luck," she said. "Open only when you need it."

John felt friendly enough with the other teachers at the party to talk shop, berating students and taking the occasional stab at administration, but little else. Clearly, some considered him still sensitive enough about his divorce that they avoided all talk of relationships around him. After an overextended discussion with a history teacher about bad oral presentations they had both suffered through, at a moment John found himself missing Xenia the most, he opened the envelope.

They were postcard originals, stiff with glue. One was a mass of motel signs, another a glass of chocolate milk next to a plate of hush puppies.

But what John liked best were the captions written on the back in an almost calligraphic hand:

Smell the salt.
—Love, Xenia

Our love has an atomic weight of 4.1683.
—Love, Xenia

'If Ford is to Chevrolet, what Dodge is to Chrysler, what Corn Flakes are to Post Toasties, what the clear blue sky is to the deep blue sea, what Hank Williams is to Neil Armstrong... Can you doubt we were made for each other?'
—Lyle Lovett
—Love, Xenia

It was a tidy fight and makeup—they were back together by Calvin's next visit. During the drive south, when John suggested they go to Tunnels O'Fun with Xenia, Calvin said, "We all did that last weekend." John refrained from correcting his seven year-old's English, but later, at a buffet Chinese restaurant, Calvin held up a fried wonton and said, "Thursday at Mom's, when we all had Chinese, we all had a ton of these."

John couldn't help hold back anymore. "You and your mom are not 'we all,'" he said.

"We all," Calvin said. "Me and Mom and Uncle Tim."

"You stand corrected," Xenia said. "I think you owe your son a fried wonton."

When John arrived for his next pick-up, Dawn was curiously early. She was dressed in beachwear, a couple of beach chairs tied to the luggage rack.

John couldn't help but ask. "Going somewhere?" It was morning, so there was hardly anyone in sight, much less someone he could have labeled Uncle Tim.

Dawn grabbed her hat by its wide brim and pulled it even lower onto her head. John didn't know what it was about that pose that set off such nostalgia in him, but he noticed all over again the wonderfully bright tint to Dawn's hair, her smooth skin, her gift for lipstick. He was surprised there hadn't already been an Uncle Scott, an Uncle Paul or an Uncle Bruce.

"Long Branch for the weekend," she answered.

"Alone?" He couldn't help but enjoy the edge he had on her, trying to make her reveal what he already knew and she didn't want to say.

Dawn always said she never liked lying. When she came close to it, she preferred not saying anything at all. In the meantime, Calvin transferred to John's car and strapped himself into his seat. John saluted, waited for Calvin to order him at ease, then asked Dawn, "Any instructions?" He almost felt bad for jibing her, but it was nice to see her so defensive. It made him feel like they could have an amicable relationship again. But when she again chose not to respond, he simply got back in his car. As he backed out of his spot, Dawn blew Calvin a kiss, though the boy was studying the dashboard since he was teaching himself how to drive.

But before he was out of the parking lot, John saw a man in a tank top and cut-off jeans lean out the front door of the Burger King. He was tall, tan, and windswept, and he was making sure the coast was clear. John tooted his horn.

"Say so long to Uncle Tim," he said to Calvin, and together the two of them waved. John was surprised how sincerely friendly he felt as he smiled. Uncle Tim managed a smile back.

With the school year almost over, John had a lot of essays to grade, so he spent most of his time at Xenia's. Though she proved to be a distraction at times, the distractions were more pleasant than if he were at his own place and talking himself into cleaning jobs to keep away from his work.

Then, one morning, shortly after John had turned in his grades and had not yet planned out his summer, Xenia woke him by dropping a change of clothes onto his chest and pulling his ear. She had a camera around her neck and her car keys jingling in her hand.

"Come on," she said as though for the hundredth time.

She drove along a few back roads, deep into a stretch of bull pines, where the roads no longer had signs. Xenia drove well under the limit.

John leaned forward on the dashboard and watched the sun through the branches of the short trees. It was nice to be on the road, and John was fine with not knowing where they were going. As long as they were back by Friday night so he could be up early to get Calvin.

After another half an hour, with no end to the area they were in, Xenia pulled over. "It's around here, I think," she said as she jiggled the stick into neutral and pulled up the emergency brake. She grabbed her backpack from the back seat and set out into the woods.

John watched from the car at first, but as Xenia started to wander out of sight, he got out and followed her.

Xenia called out, "Where is John's tree?" She walked up to one, its branches within jumping reach. She leaned against it and looked up as a small child would to a giant.

"Are you?" she called loudly, as though the tree could hear only at its very tip. She moved on to another, a wider one with a thicker array of branches, then on to four more, all the while John staying just a few paces back. He had an urge to go to each rejected tree and ask it, "Whose tree are you, then?"

It was the one with sagging branches and a thick bed of brown, hard needles underneath, that she didn't even ask. She just leaned with her back against it, her arms reaching behind her as if that were John himself, nibbling on her ear. She looked so pretty—her eyes closed, strands of black, black hair hanging in her face, her experienced hands finding fissures in the bark.

But as John approached her, she suddenly broke from the tree and squirmed out of her backpack. It fell with a heavy thunk. She took out a hammer and a box of cement nails. She started hammering one into the tree.

"Gimme a shock," she said, an extra nail between her teeth.

"Huh?"

"Shock, shock," she demanded. She pointed the hammer at his feet.

John sat on the bed of needles and took off one of his shoes. He rolled down the thick white sock with a W on the side, then got up quickly to brush off the dead needles pricking his rear. He gave the sock to Xenia, and she hung it from the nail. She stepped back and admired her work.

He hugged her from behind, and she responded by pressing into him. "Where's your tree?" he asked.

She waved out behind them, the head of the hammer nearly striking John in the hip. He wondered if she meant across the road or just close to his.

It wasn't long before they crossed a river and passed from the sandy soil and stunted trees of the Pine Barrens into hilly, green and large Pennsylvania. They stopped for gas, which John got to pump for himself. Afterwards, back on the road, Xenia reached over him and went for the glove compartment. She took out a postcard, an ad for Stevie Ray Vaughan and Double Trouble's *Greatest Hits*. Xenia took it and her Bic and used the steering wheel as her writing pad. She scrawled, then drew carefully, then scrawled, then handed it over.

'John & Xenia.'

He could barely make out the names, but the ampersand was clear and exquisite. He took her hand from the steering wheel. He held it for a while, then slid the postcard into his chest pocket. He smiled at her and squeezed her hand twice.

She yanked him toward her, the car drifting into the other lane. "The needs of the many," she cried out as she pulled the postcard from his pocket and held it out her window. It wobbled loudly before it flew from her hand.

John turned in his seat and watched the postcard swoop and dip before disappearing into the forest anonymity.

Xenia looked proud of herself.

When the sun was ready to set, they stopped at a motel called The Cabins, John had no idea where. While an old man in a hunting cap checked them in, John threw back a few cups of water from the cooler. When they got to the room with its tasseled bedspread and generic mallard-in-flight painting, Xenia flopped onto the bed and John took the easy chair. He put his head back and thought he might take a quick nap before dinner, but then Xenia slipped onto his lap, as fluidly as an affectionate cat. She handed him a photograph: a nude in a garden, circa 1920, standing on her toes, hands to her hat, as though her only concern were a sudden gust of wind. The spot of pubic hair was inky black.

"Those were great breasts then," Xenia said. She sighed like a nostalgic old woman. "Don't make them like that anymore."

John took one of her breasts in his hand and felt it clinically. From it, he looked down to the breasts of the past.

"Don't worry," Xenia said. "I'm getting them replaced." He gave her breasts a quick lift and let them fall. John wouldn't have been surprised if they had come off altogether, fallen down through her shirt and plopped onto the floor, where they would have rolled along like water balloons.

"Replaced?" he asked, frowning—he would miss these breasts.

She nodded. Leaning back and using John's knees for support, she swung her leg over so she was facing him now. John reached out and placed a boyish grip on her breasts—no pressure, his hands cupped around them gently as though holding pickled eggs.

Night darkened the room steadily, and in phases they got each other's clothes off. John usually felt spied on in hotel rooms, but Xenia was too passionate for him to consider anything but her. Afterward, she slid her arms around his neck and hugged him so hard he thought he would suffocate in her sweat-dampened hair. His chest and back were bruised in the places she'd pinched him, pulling him along for more, and he could feel the glisten on her arms mingling with his on the back of his neck. She whispered to him:

"Il a fait de sa fille une divinitè—mieux encore une chareresse, quie se cache, dit-on, ainsi qu'une déesse dans ce doux paradis aux profanes fermé."

He took her hand and kissed the fingertips. "Oui," he said, and she seemed satisfied with that response.

All night, interrupted only by moments of sleep he wouldn't realize until the next morning, he watched the ceiling, the washes of light from passing cars, and her name, the flower, spelled phonetically, float in an asymmetrical orbit. He felt such an easiness about him, a feeling of some kind of consummation.

They had breakfast at a buffet place visited mostly by pickup trucks. Ham, eggs, biscuits, gravy, and the waitress with a vacant look and wide smile brought toast on request. Xenia almost threw a spat when the waitress said she wouldn't bring four plates of toast at one time.

"I'm eventually going to have four," Xenia argued. "I can munch toast all day, you watch me."

In defiance, toast was all she ate, six plates of four diagonally cut slices washed down with milk. She only went to the buffet table to give herself an excuse to stand next to a one-armed man who was preparing a plate of ham and one biscuit. John feared she was going to ask the man how he pulled on his pants in the morning, but she only watched as he balanced his plate on the edge of the ham bin, carefully spread ham slices evenly to avoid tipping, then place the biscuit delicately in the center. Finally, John caught her nudging the man's empty sleeve with her elbow. He made her leave behind her plate, which had only a token spoonful of white and yellow runny egg, and sat her down. She glared at John for a while, but he ignored her until she stopped. When the waitress came back, Xenia greeted her warmly and thanked her for the toast.

Then John announced, "So it's nine-thirty. We start back now, we can get home by, what? Five, maybe? Six, tops?" It was Friday. There was Calvin to pick up the next morning. He had to be on the road by seven. Any later, and he'd hit traffic up around Barnegat, then arrive late with Dawn glowering and ready to yell at him.

"Pshaw," she said, rolling up her eyes, refusing to look at him. She scanned the room, purposefully moving over his presence. She nibbled at the crust of a toast sandwich.

"It's Friday, you know." He wanted to keep driving, but there were things he had to do. "I have to be home tonight, early morning at the latest."

"Who says?" she said, brown crumbs falling from her lips.

He didn't want to argue about this. "I just have to," he said. "I wish I had a choice, but all this was decided a long time ago. Some things we just have to live with and do even though we don't want to." All too late, he realized he was making a speech.

Xenia shrugged and looked out the window. She nodded as though someone were whispering in her ear, I told you so.

They drove back without saying much. Every now and then, Xenia read aloud storefronts and road signs in a slow voice, as if trying to make them sound funny. John was unshowered and hot, sweat rolling along the inside of his shirt. He felt disgusting and old, but he took comfort that Xenia let him put his hand on her knee, except when she had to get into fifth gear.

Within a week Xenia was gone. John left her two messages, which went unanswered, then her number was no longer in service. John went by her apartment, but was met by Xenia's landlord, a brooding woman who looked awful in flower prints. She complained to John about stuff left behind: dirty clothes, twenty cans of tuna fish, and bags and bags of shredded paper. But there were no postcards, and it was one of those John wanted the most. Calvin stopped asking about her within a couple of visits. Dawn kept asking him in concerned tones if he was going to be all right (could she have known that John had made frequent trips by Xenia's, hoping for a light in the window?), but John kept telling himself that Xenia had just gone away to be by herself for a bit.

He could never imagine Xenia in a specific place, but every now and then he would picture her cuddling up to some younger man, and John would hit his pillow. He went to bookstores and searched through the postcard racks, anything for a lead, but he never found anything attributed to her. She had floated away from him, like a pleasing smell you'd like to dwell on—when it's gone, there's no hope of finding it again.

John played out the rest of the summer working on a rowboat he bought for fifty dollars and the stipulation that he drag it out of the junkyard himself. It was a decrepit, wooden thing, and John knew he'd never make it seaworthy, but it was something to do. He rented a landlocked garage. He spent money he didn't have on power tools, and he worked every day to exhaustion, all the while knowing he would never finish, never finish, never finish. When Calvin was there, he let the boy play inside the imperfect hull. Calvin's favorite game was to reach like a sea anemone over the side and sting his father's shoulder.

It had been years since John had done any kind of handiwork, but it was remarkable how quickly two years of high school shop returned to him, the lessons learned making jewelry boxes and wooden nameplates and tic-tac-toe boards. In brief, fleeting moments, he convinced himself this boat had to be perfect, and though Xenia would have scoffed at him and told him that the only perfection would have been not to have a boat at all, still he worked at it, and sometimes, when his arms were tired from pushing the leveler, keeping reign on the sander, his mind drifted to Xenia. He talked to her of boat building, though she always ignored him and studied her earrings, which pulled on her lobes dangerously.

"I'm busy," she'd tell him.

But he didn't think of her often. Only when he believed he'd caught a whiff of her Jergen's, the Aqua Net, her raspberry lipstick. He was pleased more with a hard day's work, the thick layers of sawdust that never completely washed off, the fumes of sealant embedded deep in his shirt, the peaceful mind he carried when he finally went inside for his first beer of the evening. As the summer ended, he looked forward to the school year. A new bunch of names, a crowd of students he had to get to know from scratch. On Labor Day, he lovingly tarped the rowboat, which he never named, and felt like an initiate into the world of cluttered back yards.

In his dreams, Xenia always had large, white hands.

Richard Weems

REAL GRIEF

Mrs. Jonathan Brown of Rockville, Maryland, thought the Victorians had it right: grief was a physiological manifestation arising from emotional trauma, yet inseparable from its physical displays. Grief was wearing black or properly somber colors to a funeral and expressing socially appropriate condolences to the surviving family. Proper grief involved tears and fits of sorrow and longing looks at the deceased's embalmed corpse. Grief exhibited empirical symptoms: headaches, asthma, rheumatism, ulcerative colitis. Grief was man's one capacity that elevated him above the animals. "You'll never see a viewing at an Elephant's Graveyard," Mrs. Brown was fond of saying.

Mrs. Brown began her studies in grief after her husband's funeral three years ago. Jonathan had died of natural causes, a cardiac arrest caused by prolonged high blood pressure, and Mrs. Brown found herself unable to grieve for him at his services and burial. Her grown sons and their families came, a slew of people at the house, all of whom took turns grasping her hand or hugging her or kissing her cheek, all of them full of condolences, but Mrs. Brown felt little but the urge to send everyone away and leave her alone. Eventually, they did.

From there, Mrs. Brown she decided to learn all she could about grief. She read books written by self-proclaimed experts, but Mrs. Brown's true knowledge of grief was the product of visiting funeral parlors with Mrs. LaRe. Mrs. LaRe's husband was Irving LaRe, the most successful mortician in Montgomery County. Mrs. Brown drove Mrs. LaRe, who couldn't work a clutch because of the pin in her left hip, to other funeral parlors so she could observe and critique the practices of other morticians and relate her findings to her husband. Between her years of experience in attending funerals and the volume of trade secrets concerning the mortuary business that Mrs. LaRe had revealed to her during their association, Mrs. Brown had no doubt concerning her expertise, and at the first day for viewing Ethan Edward Climie in the Gold Room of Sutter's Funeral Home in Severna Park, Mrs. Brown noticed a remarkable young man sitting across the aisle from her.

What Mrs. Brown first admired about this young man was his fine display of grief. She arrived with Mrs. LaRe at Sutter's only twenty minutes after the doors to the Gold Room had opened, but when they entered, this young man was already seated and crying, his eyes a deep red, his nose running. He was wearing an appropriately dark-grey jacket and black pants. He had one hand in the pocket of his jacket. His crepe tie was a deep black, like a strip of dark matter down his chest.

Mrs. Brown concluded this man to be the Clifford Donne whose name topped the guest register in the lobby. Mr. Gregory Tallis and Wife, Heather, were the couple two rows in front of Mrs. Brown and Mrs. LaRe. Heather Tallis's dress was a suspiciously unsomber shade of brown, light enough to appear almost tan, but since she was on the verge of crying herself, no doubt inspired by the loud sniffles and grunting sobs of Clifford Donne, Mrs. Brown did not think too poorly of her. Mrs. Ian McFarlan was the middle-aged woman with wide hips on one knee before the widow at the front of the room, speaking in hushed whispers with Mrs. Climie. Mrs. Climie sat at the foot of her deceased husband's solid-oak half-couch with gold taffeta lining that matched the flanking marigold display. Mrs. Climie's sable dress was a deep black, as was her wide-brimmed hat and full-length veil. The veil was so dark it seemed opaque. She sat obediently, her back bent as though from the weight of her sorrow, her insides aching from the effects of her grief, possibly, and Mrs. Brown glowed with pride at the sight of this. When she turned, her eyes met Clifford Donne's, and she nodded to him, pleased to be in the vicinity of such fine representations of grief. Clifford Donne suddenly looked nervous, as if he had been caught at the scene of a crime.

Mrs. LaRe shifted in her seat. "Ooh, my hip," she grumbled, sliding back and forth. When she finally settled in, her sigh of relief mingling with the air escaping the cushion of her seat, she put on her eyeglasses, which she kept on a chain around her neck. She looked around carefully through the tortoiseshell frames at the Gold Room. She squinted approvingly at the gold-colored sconces on the walls and scowled at the flecked wallpaper, which was off-white and adorned with vertical rows of gold fleurs-de-lis.

"Gaudy," she whispered to Mrs. Brown.

Mrs. Brown leaned in close to Mrs. LaRe, Clifford Donne still watching her. "Yes it is," she agreed. It was her job to remind Mrs. LaRe of her criticisms when she reported them back to Mr. LaRe over Earl Grey tea in their kitchen.

Mrs. LaRe continued with her criticism. "You could go blind in this room. Fleurs-de-lis? Never seen that before. The lobby looked good, that gray Oriental rug, but this room is far too much."

Mrs. Brown listened closely. She greatly admired the LaRes and the fine job they had done on her husband at his funeral. Mrs. Brown appreciated the appropriateness of the colors at a LaRe-prepared funeral: the blacks and grays and ivories. She also appreciated the art of embalming, and she thought Irving LaRe was the best practitioner she had ever seen. Proof of this was at the funeral for Roger Nielsen, who died last November on West 705 in a collision with an eighteen-wheeler full of milk. The Ford station wagon was totaled, but Roger Nielsen looked whole and unmarred at his funeral. Mrs. Brown was barely able to see the effects of the Flextone in Roger Nielsen's face.

Clifford Donne still stared at Mrs. Brown. Mrs. Brown tried only to ignore him.

"All those bright colors are risky," Mrs. LaRe whispered. "They usually make the corpse look very dull in comparison, very pale and lifeless." She leaned forward in her chair, the aluminum creaking under her weight, and looked toward the front of the room. She squinted some, then sat back, shaking her head.

"I'll have to check later," she whispered.

Mrs. Brown nodded, but she worried Clifford Donne might have overheard Mrs. LaRe. It was barely a month since the two women were asked to leave an outdoor service in Deale for 'disturbing the proceedings.' The surviving family scowled at them (looks full of damnation) as they were escorted out, and Mrs. Brown still could not understand why her and Mrs. LaRe's presence had been so upsetting. It was why they only attended viewings now: there was less likelihood of trouble. Deale was an experience she wanted to keep from happening again, and Mrs. Brown hoped that ignoring Clifford Donne would make him lose interest in her.

Mrs. Brown looked to the front of the room, to the Widow Climie. Mrs. McFarlan was still on one knee, holding the widow's hand in both of hers. Mrs. Climie's face was invisible behind the thick, black veil. Mrs. McFarlan spoke in whispers, and the thick, black veil nodded. Heather Tallis put her finger to her lips and looked to her husband, Gregory, her eyes brimming with tears. Gregory took her hand and rested it on her lap, his head bowed.

Mrs. LaRe took a crumpled white handkerchief from her rectangular black purse and coughed into it. In the corner of her sight, Mrs. Brown saw Clifford Donne's head follow Mrs. LaRe's hand as she put the handkerchief back. Mrs. LaRe said, "It is a fine-looking coffin, though. Batesville. You don't see many in solid oak anymore."

Mrs. Brown saw Clifford Donne take his hand from his pocket and hold it to his nose. He sniffled, and suddenly Heather Tallis started crying herself. Her shoulders shook, and she pinched the bridge of her nose. Gregory Tallis put his hand on his wife's back, by the shoulder blade, and rubbed in tight circles.

Mrs. Brown glanced towards Clifford Donne to see if he still stared at her, and she found the young man smiling, his eyes still red, his nose running. Clifford Donne smiled as if he knew something about Mrs. Brown and wanted her to know it. He raised his eyebrows, then winked. Mrs. Brown wondered if anyone had seen, but Mrs. LaRe was still looking over the coffin. The Tallises were facing the front of the room, and Mrs. McFarlan and Mrs. Climie were still in intense conversation.

Clifford Donne's stare scared Mrs. Brown. She felt a need to defend herself.

"I just want to watch," she whispered so quietly that no one could have heard. "I'm not hurting anybody. I only want to watch. That's not bad, is it?"

There was no pity in Clifford Donne's face. He was still smiling, and he cocked his head toward Heather Tallis. Heather Tallis had composed herself, but Gregory still rubbed her back. Clifford Donne sniffled, as if in demonstration, and nodded toward the Tallises again. Mrs. Brown didn't understand, and she shook her head.

Clifford Donne took a container from the pocket of his jacket and held it to his nose. A tiny cannister, the lid to which he popped up deftly with his thumb. He sniffed at it, the sniff masked as a convincing sniffle. He winced and slipped the container back into his jacket pocket. His eyes immediately began to well, and he smiled impishly at Mrs. Brown. A tear raced along the top of his cheek. His nose ran, and he sniffled it back, all the while pointing at Mrs. Brown, as if he were greeting a colleague, as if to say, "We do the same thing."

It took everything Mrs. Brown was to keep her in her seat and not stand up and expose this faker, this betrayal to real grief, but she decided to keep calm and tell Mrs. LaRe.

Mrs. LaRe was looking at the ceiling, grimacing slightly. When Mrs. Brown nudged her with her elbow, Mrs. LaRe whispered, "There's sand in the ceiling," still grimacing.

Mrs. Brown pointed across the aisle, but her friend failed to notice.

"They've sanded the ceiling," Mrs. LaRe continued. "I bet they haven't even water-sealed up there, and they've gone and sanded the ceiling. One good rainstorm, and that ceiling's going to soak right through."

"Look there," Mrs. Brown whispered forcefully.

Clifford Donne took his hand out of his pocket again, the tears on his face drying. To the naive, he could have been merely wiping his nose, but Mrs. Brown knew Mrs. LaRe's trained eye would not miss the canister of snuff or smelling salts in Clifford Donne's hand. She was sure Mrs. LaRe would be as appalled as she was at this fraud. Clifford Donne sniffed and closed his eyes tight. His whole head turned red, even the scalp.

Mrs. LaRe nodded briefly and faced front again. "Yes," she said quietly, sounding annoyed.

Clifford Donne opened his eyes again, and they were bloodshot.

"This is appalling," Mrs. Brown whispered in Mrs. LaRe's ear. "It's a disgrace. We have to speak to someone."

"It's working," Mrs. LaRe said. Heather Tallis was crying again, and even Gregory Tallis covered his mouth. Mrs. McFarlan and Mrs. Climie embraced.

Mrs. LaRe looked pleased. "It's an old trick," she said. "A little out of date, but still very effective when used properly."

Mrs. Brown bit her lower lip. Mrs. McFarlan gave the widow's hand a final squeeze and left along the outer edge of the seats, her head bowed. The Tallises rose from their seats in unison and approached the veiled Mrs. Climie, who reached out with a hand, gloved in elbow-length black cloth.

The Tallises bowed their heads respectfully as they passed the coffin. Clifford Donne faked another sob, but this one sounded more like a choked-back giggle to Mrs. Brown.

She decided she was going to tell Mrs. Climie about Clifford Donne. Surely the widow wouldn't put up with such an atrocity against real grief, this crime against deep-felt emotion, and would complain wholeheartedly to the management. Mrs. Brown thought it best she allow the Tallises to offer their condolences before she exposed the impostor.

Heather Tallis got onto one knee, and she squeezed the Mrs. Climie's hand. "If you need anything," she said, "call us. Call us for anything."

"Anything," Gregory Tallis said, leaning over his wife. His voice had a tone of finality, the way a person says, "All right," over the telephone when conversation is coming to an end. Mrs. Brown prepared to stand, and she noticed that Clifford Donne had already risen and was standing over her. Clifford Donne was smiling and holding the container from his pocket in her face.

"You better get you some tears going," he said, smirking. He had a twang to his voice—Georgia maybe. "Run some that mascara there." Mrs. Brown could read the words JOHNSON SMITH SNEEZING POWDER on the container. There were comic-strip balloons saying, ACHOO! and KER-CHOO! and HACK!, and Mrs. Brown nearly fell backwards as she tried to avoid inhaling any of the powder.

"It good powder," Clifford Donne said. "Don't smell so bad, but got some kick. Makes you eyes sting like bitches. Go on, there's plenty." He was talking in the hushed tone Mrs. Brown and Mrs. LaRe used when on the job.

Mrs. LaRe turned, looked at the sneezing powder, and smiled at Clifford Donne. "Thank you, young man," she said, quietly, "but it's not for us right now."

Gregory Tallis helped his wife up from the floor and led her down the aisle.

"We must go up front now," Mrs. LaRe said to Clifford Donne, looking past Mrs. Brown as though she were not there, though still offering her arm in a request for assistance. "Thank you, but we must go up front now."

The usual plan was for Mrs. Brown to distract the surviving family while Mrs. LaRe examined the quality of the corpse. This let Mrs. Brown compliment the survivors on a lovely service as she observed up close those in the throes of deep grief, but Mrs. Brown could not take any more. She did not want to help Mrs. LaRe down any more aisles, nor struggle with her friend's excessive weight leaning heavily on her arm. She got up and went past Clifford Donne and pushed her way past the Tallises, who were walking slowly and almost didn't see her coming. Mrs. Brown kept her eyes on the widow, who was sitting with her head practically at her chest, her hands folded in her lap, waiting patiently. Mrs. Brown turned back to see if Clifford Donne were making his escape, but he was helping Mrs. LaRe up from her seat.

"Thank you," Mrs. LaRe mumbled. Clifford Donne waited patiently, Mrs. LaRe pulling heavily on his arm. He seemed able to handle Mrs. LaRe's bulk. "It's my hip," Mrs. LaRe said. "I can't jump around like I used to as a girl. I can't do that at all."

Clifford Donne nodded understandingly. "My momma got a hip like that," he said. "Hurt her so bad, she cain't get out of bed when it raining." He helped Mrs. LaRe into the aisle, and the two started toward Mrs. Brown together, Mrs. LaRe pulling hard on Clifford Donne's arm when she hobbled on her bad hip.

"My friend I came with usually helps me," Mrs. LaRe said. "You saw her. She went on without me." Clifford Donne nodded and frowned, as if realizing what a loss this was.

"This parlor you have here is a little gaudy in some ways," she said, "but a good atmosphere. It's really somber in its own ways." As she talked, she waved her free hand in the air, motioning to nothing in particular. It was the motion she always used when telling Mrs. Brown about the funeral business, and Mrs. Brown suddenly felt alone, as she did at Jonathan's funeral. "What's your name, young man?"

"Clifford Donne," Clifford Donne said. "I don't run the place none. I'm a cousin of Sutter's, the-guy-who-owns-the-parlor Sutter. I sleep in the storage room 'til I can afford myself my own place up here. I like them steel coffins the best. They're cool this time of the year."

Mrs. Brown turned and stepped up to Mrs. Climie. She felt comfortable here. She was a widow herself. This close, she could see through the veil over Mrs. Climie's face.

Mrs. Climie was an old, old woman, much older than Ethan Climie, it seemed. She held out her black-gloved hand, reaching for one of Mrs. Brown's hands. Her make-up was heavy and smeared; she looked terrible and inhuman. Her eyes were red and puffy, tears still welling and falling and dripping from her face.

This was not grief. It looked like grief, all the symptoms were present, but there was something else in Mrs. Climie's look, something Mrs. Brown knew nothing about, and it scared her. Mrs. Climie looked desperate for a hand to grasp, and she shook her head as if trying to tell Mrs. Brown that she was going to scream if she didn't have that hand soon, she would go mad, jump up and take that hand by force and start laughing, and if she did, Mrs. Brown was sure she was never going to stop. She tried to wave Mrs. Climie away, but the widow continued to reach for her hand, and Mrs. Brown felt as though she were trying to fend off poisonous snakes. She feared for her very life.

Mrs. LaRe was leaning on the coffin, examining Ethan Climie inside, nodding and saying to herself, "Nice work. Yes, yes, very nice workmanship." Clifford Donne stood by and, with arms crossed, grinned to himself as if proud to be watching such an expert at work. Mrs. LaRe patted Ethan Edward Climie on the cheek to check the rigidity. She was careful to pat lightly enough so as to not mar the rouge.

Richard Weems

A MURDER DURING THE REAGAN ERA

The village of Yellow Birch in the Adirondack foothills started as Yellow Birch Lumber and Furnishings, a post-WWII saw mill and furniture factory situated along an isolated stretch of Plank Road off route 812. Beaver River lay on one side, an anonymous mound-like hill on the other. Proprietor and foreman Ole Knussen, a deserter from the Swedish navy who lost half of his left hand while a lumberjack in Canada, built an orchard of houses around his business so he could demand long hours of his workers and pay them little. Ole himself kept a cot and a mug full of toiletries in his office—the only thing he couldn't sleep through was the sound of quota not being met. His father died behind the plow back in the old country, and when he admonished his workers he told them how his blind grandmother stirred lye for a Stockholm laundry service well into her eighties. Every worker at some point got chastised by Ole for being lazy.

"Toil," he'd admonish. Then he'd poke at the pink flesh where his ring finger used to be. "Toil makes a man a man and a woman useful."

For almost thirty years, lumber flowed down Beaver River from Canada; straddle chairs and coffee tables trucked north by the convoy. Yellow Birch Lumber and Furnishings fared well enough for Ole to bring in more workers. He built more houses, all clones of the first down to the kitchen linoleum and cabinet hardware, and a rooming house for the bachelors. Yellow Birch grew four side streets. A Methodist church popped up along Plank Road, as well as a butcher shop, a tavern, an IGA, a hardware store, even a gas station. Cale Keefer and Nathan Grimbley quit the mill in the 70s to start an eatery as well as a combined Laundromat and liquor store. Pearson Natterly bought up a stretch of acreage just outside the village and planted corn. Nolt Huck acquired his own stretch to start a cow farm. Ole offered fair deals on his land, maybe to give him even more reason to complain to his workers if they requested time off to go to Croghan or Watertown.

"I give you shelter," he'd say as he mussed his beard and waved his hands at the houses around him, "for what? So you can vacation and get me behind schedule?"

The folk of Yellow Birch may not have agreed with their boss, but still they put in the hours asked of them. After all, they had shelter, money for food and all the firewood they could carry.

But then, at the tail end of the Carter administration, the interstates took over the lumber routes, and Plank Road, bumpy as hell from decades of cheap patchwork, downgraded to a minor route for loggers looking to skirt lumber restrictions. Ole Knussen convinced his floor supervisor, Randy Pellernate, to buy him out of the saw mill, but lumber shipments were too few and far between for Randy to keep anyone on a steady salary. No one was fool enough to buy into the furniture factory, where chairs and tables stockpiled into a fire hazard. Ole, a bachelor septuagenarian, moved to New Jersey and married a former Polish beauty queen, who blew through his savings and divorced him in under a year. Ole Knussen spent his retirement selling Amway door to door while his former employees fell on tight times.

Some families moved south to Lowville to work in the bowling pin factory or the Kraft cheese plant, but most folks hired themselves out as cash workers in neighboring towns or farms. Nolt Huck and Pearson Natterly took on as many hands as they could, but their needs were not large enough. Each dawn triggered a mass exodus of pick-ups that didn't return to Yellow Birch until after dark. Households shared their pantries and dinner tables with those having a harder time to get by, and Del Throaton at the IGA extended long lines of credit. Molly Fishkill, who had taken over the rooming house and dubbed it the Roger Arms after her departed husband, charged her regular residents only what she needed to keep the lights running and the heat on. The surplus furniture in the abandoned factory quickly disappeared into wood stoves, and the work tables made good patches for sagging walls and floors. The machinery was gutted for makeshift engine parts, and the look-alike houses faded to a mere speckle of the yellows and powder blues Ole Knussen had christened them with. Propane tanks rusted on their stands until they tilted like grounded submarines. Sometimes, the only members of a family who could expect balanced meals were the school kids, but they usually dropped out of Beaver Central and went to work before they were seventeen.

But then, early in the Reagan administration, a novice map-reader for the Postal Service mistook Yellow Birch for a burgeoning metropolis and awarded it its own zip code and the federal funding to put together a postal staff. The businessmen formed a town council that met at the tavern, the Sawdust. Bill Williams, the butcher, declared himself mayor, and he was a thick enough man for his declaration to go unopposed. He ordered one of the factory storage sheds refurbished into a PO, and nominated two locals, Margaret Satchel and Jesse Champee, for federal employment. Jesse's parents were among the original group of Yellow Birch employees, and he had twenty years of factory work under his own belt when Ole Knussen closed shop, so no one begrudged the fifty year-old the paycheck that came with his mailbag.

But Margaret Satchel was a different story. Ten years before, she had refused to quit high school, even when her father broke his ankle under a hay baler. The only thing she did with her diploma was to take a part-time job behind the counter of Bill Williams's butcher shop and fritter away her wages on manicures, hairstyles and wardrobe. Yellow Birch's first mayor insisted that Margaret kept his shop running as smoothly as a well-lubed slicer, but as a government employee, Margaret kept short, sporadic hours. The PO was liable to close up and go dark at any time of the day, a crumpled sheet of lined notebook paper taped inside the window announcing RIGHT BACK. Still, getting mail in town proved a lot easier than waiting for the once-a-week delivery from Croghan (longer, if the roads were bad), so inconvenient hours were nothing worth making a stink over.

With the one-digit zip code distinction from Croghan came reporters from *The Utica Observer* and Channel 7 Watertown. Yellow Birch folk had no ill-will against these strangers, but they had little desire to talk into cameras or have their words put into print, so when the Utica reporter stepped into the Sawdust to get reactions from the drinking men, most of the regulars offered little more than reticent, noncommittal movements of the head and comments about the weather. But Stu Clutterbuck, always a bit of a wise-ass when he had a few in him, pulled on the bill of his orange cap and wondered aloud if he would be able to get his mail over there at the new PO.

"Do you think they'll even let me send things out?" he said to the unamused journalist. "Like, to Lowville, or even farther? Does the post office charge by the mile?"

The only one to get into both the article and the 11 p.m. broadcast was Molly Fishkill, who converted the shed next to the Roger Arms into a library in an effort to boost town morale. In one breath, she not only offered her gratitude to president Reagan (for whom she had voted) for recognizing Yellow Birch's independence, as it were, but her annoyance at the Croghan post office and her pride at now being able to lend out three hundred and twenty-six books, thanks to donations from Beaver Central. She even managed to slide in a plug for the Roger Arms, a good layover for drivers taking the scenic route to Canada or vice-versa. For days after her first TV appearance, Molly walked with a lighter step, as though she'd been pumped full of helium.

Molly's verbosity proved worthwhile, as Plank Road became a scenic alternative for those coming south for the raceway in New Bremen. Track fans came through almost any time of year, whether for snowmobile heats, motorcycle enduros, or the 76-lap ASA Challenger Late Model Twin 25's. Bill Williams's secret recipe bologna became a popular item for race day tailgate parties, and Bill and his wife, Trudy, made up a sheet of recipes to sell for a quarter: baked bologna on a saltine with Muenster, bologna kabob with onions and string beans, creamed bologna on toast, etc. Cale Keefer and Nathan Grimbley added an ice cream counter to their eatery and changed its name from the Village Eatery to the Dog & Cream. Regular folk still had to travel all over to find work, but the post office had apparently brought some life back to Yellow Birch.

Unfortunately, it would also bring about Yellow Birch's first murder.

The unfortunate part of Jesse Champee's federal job was that his friends and neighbors wanted to keep its cushy nature well hidden, as though they feared the Postmaster General would vacate Jesse's position if he knew how little work it entailed. Yellow Birch was an easy walk from end to end, even easier when behind the wheel of a USPS jeep, yet Jesse's rounds still took him a good part of the day. The older women invited him in for simple chores or for cornbread or a cup of ambrosia, and the men discussed fishing or ways to repair a fried transmission. When his lunch break came around, he would find a fried bologna sandwich waiting for him at the next house, or a foil pouch filled with rainbow trout.

But Jesse's glacial progress in making his rounds would turn out to be the final link of evidence Petunia, Jesse's wife, needed to convict her husband of infidelity. Petunia spent a good deal of time inside her house, as she saw life-threatening bacteria spilling from the mouths of friends and neighbors alike, especially those who kept free-roaming animals. Petunia was the daughter of Roy Illinois, a former bandsaw operator who kept an especially rundown house at the north end of Incline Lane. His back lot was a spread of vehicles that he had scrounged off of others when they'd conked out. Every now and then he coaxed one back to life, but most ended up as the storage facilities for Petunia's mother, Elaine, who churned out macramé hats and blankets that she refused to sell or donate. Petunia had inherited her parents' hoard mentality, and Jesse sometimes snuck out during the night to return bundles of grocery bags to the IGA or toss bags of used napkins into someone else's garbage, efforts that would elicit only caterwauls from the Champee house the next day. To Petunia's mind, the only reason her husband needed several hours to deliver mail in the village was that he must have had a bevy of jezebels to service along the way. Plus, her husband now worked in regular proximity to that sleazy, easy Margaret Satchel.

In truth, Jesse did have a healthy libido for his age, but he tried his best not to fantasize about Margaret Satchel, who was thirty years younger than him and committed to an affair with Bill Williams, who found the mailbags in the back room of the PO more comfortable than his meat locker. Sometimes Jesse served as lookout while Bill and Margaret grunted and gasped as though hauling sides of beef, his libido pulsing like a geyser with a cork in it. Twenty-eight years ago, Petunia decided she could no longer stand breathing in Jesse's germs in her sleep and moved into the other bedroom, so once Margaret and Bill finished, Jesse would take the jeep down the road to a private spot where he could relieve his urges. But even these jaunts out of the village fueled Petunia's condemnation as she imagined the woods home to feral, naked hussies craving her husband's fluids.

Petunia was a little nervous when she served Jesse his first bowl of corn chowder and Peak antifreeze, but Jesse merely remarked how sweet the soup was, and could he have some more water? The next day, he looked a little wan, but he passed it off as the ill effects of a bad night's sleep. Days went by when he couldn't keep much solid food down, and after a few stops on his route, he had to sit in his jeep until he could recover enough wind to trudge up to a couple more houses. He turned down soup and ambrosia, and the smell of Bill Williams's bologna made him woozy. Still, he insisted that he had nothing more than a stomach bug.

"I knew that potato was rotten," he'd mumble and chuckle as he hobbled back to his jeep.

On his worst days, when the pain in his gut was so bad that he couldn't get out of bed, folk came to the post office for their mail. This sudden surge of business usually flustered Margaret, who'd lament aloud about how useless an employee Jesse was, but then Petunia marched into the PO one day while Jesse was out and pointed a crooked finger at the waxed spot between Margaret's eyebrows.

"You bust up our home enough as it is," Petunia said, aiming her venom down that finger and straight into Margaret's brain. Delores Clatterturn and Little Alfred Liddell each took a step back to give Petunia room to spew. "I'll take care of things on my end, so don't you make a stink and lose my Jesse his job and his life insurance."

Margaret was normally not one to take commands, but Petunia's glare was as piercing as an awl, and slowly Margaret acquiesced. When Delores and Little Alfred finally got their mail, they couldn't help but notice the aftershock tremoring throughout Margaret's manicured hands.

When Jesse's illness went into its third month, folk worried that he might have been under the influence of something a little stronger than the stomach flu. The nearest doctor was in Boonville, the nearest hospital in Watertown, so anything less than an emergency was usually waded through with aspirin and home remedies. Lucinda Pearl brought some ginger-barley tea to the Champee house when Jesse had been laid up for three days straight, but Petunia insisted that her corn chowder was all her husband needed.

"Jesse breaks out in hives at the sight of ginger," Petunia insisted.

When Jesse did get back to work, after a week in bed, he had to rest at every house and barely finished before quitting time. Martin Cuthery drove Jesse home and offered to take him to Watertown, but Petunia of course balked.

"What if they find a cancer?" she said. "Where will we be then? What if they find an incurable venereal disease? Will it do any good to know for sure that he's on his death bed?" She took Jesse by the arm and helped him out of the cab. "Corn chowder," she said. "All you need is more corn chowder, my sick thing."

But Jesse's eyes rolled up into his head, and he fainted on the porch. A line of bile ran from the corner of his mouth. Martin Cuthery carried Jesse back to his truck after inching past Petunia and brought Jesse to Mercy Hospital. Jesse went through several tests and waited for a pronouncement of cancer, but anyone's best guess was food poisoning, some mayonnaise gone bad or a rotten sardine. A couple of hours on an IV perked him up, but he deteriorated once he got back home for dinner. When he wanted to get back to the hospital, he left straight from work, since Petunia would have only pushed more corn chowder on him.

So off and on, over the course of a year, Jesse would go to the hospital every three months or so when he felt particularly bad, and after some treatment and fluids he would come back home, only to get sick again. Petunia had a hard time keeping most of her thoughts to herself, and more than once she told others that she was glad her husband was so sick, because he no longer had the energy to prance through the field with Margaret Satchel or any of the other dozens of women who catered to his delights.

"No sluts for him," she'd say, maybe while filling up the tank of their rusted truck or going through her purse to pay for light bulbs. "He don't have the gumption to stroke himself when he's in a bad state, much less the Satchel girl's petard." Folk smiled in a noncommittal fashion to these rants they were all too familiar with.

Jesse Champee died, of course, while on his route. He'd been back from Mercy Hospital only a day. He was getting up his wind to bring a parcel to Emily Nukkel, but then he put his forehead against the steering wheel, took two deep breaths, muttered something about minced meat, and exhaled for all time. Emily Nukkel rushed out, hoping to save Jesse a trip up her steps, and found the mailman's body.

Petunia would have killed Jesse much sooner, but arrangements with Suffern's Funeral Parlor in Turin had taken twelve months to pay off, and she didn't want to deal with the bills while waiting for Jesse's insurance to come through. But then Mercy Hospital flagged Jesse's death as suspicious and refused to release the body. Petunia threatened a good, old-fashioned hair-pull if Jesse's remains were not sent to Suffern's, but by then she had shut herself in completely and refused to come to the door even when neighbors came by with fresh-baked rolls or turkey pot pies to express their condolences. At night, the only light in the Champee house came from Jesse's bedroom, where Petunia sifted through Jesse's things, pulled plaster from the walls and chiseled up floorboards for physical evidence of Jesse's entanglements—unfamiliar pubic hair, a letter rife with intimate details or lascivious speech, or a pair of boxers stained with fluid. The less she found, the more she wept, for how could Jesse do this to her? How could he screw around on her and not leave her some evidence to exonerate her retribution? She slept only briefly, fifteen minutes or so at a time, and when the state troopers came with their warrant, one of them could have carried her out in a laundry basket, she was so light and frail.

And how did the folk of Yellow Birch react? Their mailman murdered, the accused one of their own? For one, Molly Fishkill organized a Petunia Champee legal defense fund. Collection cans appeared by every cash register in town, and Molly sold chocolate drop cookies so she could send

Petunia a monthly care package of Yellow Birch bologna wrapped in blue freezer packs and a loaf of fresh bread. But Molly refrained from identifying herself in the return address. Jesse's death was criminal and undeserved, and no one had any doubt about Petunia's guilt, especially when the Watertown news showed footage of her arraignment, where she cried out that her husband was "nothing better than a ripe horndog" and sneered while she grabbed her own crotch, but judgment was not theirs to make. That duty belonged to the court and the power above the court, and despite the apparent nature of her guilt, Petunia Champee was one of Yellow Birch's own, so the care packages kept going out. Some tried to drop off food and words of comfort to Roy and Elaine Illinois, but they wouldn't answer the door.

Reporters once again swept into town for exclusives and interviews, but so many this time that Molly Fishkill had to create a NO VACANCY sign for the Roger Arms, the first ever in the history of the establishment. Cale Keefer, always one to sniff a money-making opportunity, rented out cots in the Dog & Cream after closing and even threw in a hot dog and soda for a modest fee. The crews who didn't want to pay for accommodations slept in their vans and ran their engines all night against the January freeze. Still, Yellow Birch folk met their queries with friendly but unhelpful reticence.

Rather than depend on the news outlets for the events of the trial, Delores Clatterturn and Mazey Wurm made the daily trek to the county seat and reported the day's proceedings in the Lutheran church basement every evening. Expert upon expert was called by the prosecution to review charts and the chemical formula for ethylene glycol and the levels found in Jesse's blood and kidney tissue. One, a gnomish man with sad and dark eyes, even connected the half-empty gallon of Peak in the basement of the Champee house to the substance absorbed into Jesse's body (Petunia had poured in a little Kayo syrup to sweeten the stuff). But despite this damning evidence, Petunia, who wore print dresses most of the time and one day a hat and black veil pinned to the top of her hair, simply gave the judge the stink-eye or tried to pass notes on a yellow legal pad to her rumpled public defender, who wouldn't take them.

The morning that Petunia's defense was to begin, Roy and Elaine Illinois emerged onto their front porch. Roy had on the slacks, corduroy jacket and flannel sports shirt he usually wore for church, and Elaine had buttoned a sweater over the kind of flower-print dress that she had taught her daughter how to make. Each had a busted-up American Tourister in hand.

Penelope Durst, who lived across the street from the Illinois house, called out to them from her kitchen window, but neither responded. Roy and Elaine clopped down the porch steps with the deliberation of executioners. While Roy searched for a vehicle that would turn over, Elaine shaded her eyes as though from the sun (the day was overcast). Penelope called to them again and even offered them some warm banana bread, but Roy continued to turn key after key until the white Ford with the missing tailgate trembled with combustion. Elaine plopped the suitcases into the bed, and by the time Penelope had dried her hands of dishwater and stepped out of her back door, Roy and Elaine were puttering their way out of the village. Roy couldn't coax the Ford above second gear, and folk along Plank Road each put up a hand in a motionless wave, like when the Legionnaires rode through on the Croghan fire engine every Veteran's and Memorial Day.

When court convened for the day, Roy and Elaine took up spots against the far wall. Petunia was too busy aiming sour looks at the prosecution team to notice them. Mazey Wurm and Delores Clatterturn dared a friendly wave, but Roy and Elaine took no notice. They remained stoic as their daughter's lawyer made half-assed attempts to question the validity of toxicology and forensic science. Roy stared at the back of the chair in front of him and Elaine at her gloves when Petunia took the stand against advice of counsel and testified to Jesse's systematic adultery up and down each street of Yellow Birch, including the feral, naked hussies he drove down the road to be with. She spoke of the gallons of antifreeze in every basement in town and the conspiracy of trollops out to frame her. The prosecutor's only cross examination was to have the most delusional sections read back to the jury and confirmed by Petunia, who nodded avidly at the thought that someone, finally, understood her.

The verdict came in the same day, and when Petunia was found guilty of murder as well as a full page of other charges, including unsafe handling of hazardous materials, she clapped her hands and shook her head as though she had just seen a referee make a bad call at a football game. Roy and Elaine Illinois stared at the hats in their hands. Mazey tried to get to the elderly couple to express her sympathies, but the courtroom was standing room only, and Roy and Elaine made their exit without once having met their daughter's eyes.

Outside, Roy got a couple of boys to push the Ford into gear, and he and his wife chugged north and never returned to Yellow Birch. Petunia got twenty-five years. Jesse's cremated remains were sent south to Hubbardsville, where his parents had been scattered. The Yellow Birch council didn't have the heart to hire another letter carrier, so run of the post office fell solely on Margaret Satchel, whose affair with Mayor Williams cooled as she tried to keep the mail sorted and the postage inventoried and the till balanced. Molly Fishkill officially closed the Petunia Champee Defense Fund with a final package of venison jerky and cinnamon bread. She included a card full of inspirational couplets, but it went unsigned.

But Petunia Champee was too much of an oddball to fade from the village's memory. Her letters started arriving a few months into her incarceration—sometimes she sent three in one week, but then she wouldn't write again for four months. Sometimes she addressed her former neighbors, and sometimes she just wrote to Interested Parties, c/o Yellow Birch, NY. Margaret Satchel pinned the latter to the PO bulletin board for anyone to take. Every letter implored its reader to write her back immediately, especially if her letters weren't getting through due to the efforts of a "certain postal hussy" whose "untrue heart will go unnamed." Petunia would then go on for a paragraph or so about prison life and the fellow inmates who had also been wrongly prosecuted, a preamble to her continued pleas of innocence and her litany about the judge's incompetence, this man who, as she put it, had been handed the proof of her innocence and had refused to admit it into evidence, this judge who, as everyone in jail knew, sentenced the innocent and influenced juries against those he had taken a dislike to. Petunia insisted that there was a major hole in the physical evidence against her—the jury had failed to realize that "a chemical half-lifes itself until it disappears."

Petunia persisted through the years in her inconsistent way, but her handwriting was so recognizable, as was the state prison postmark, that her letters eventually became as easily discarded as prayer envelopes from southern evangelists or cologne samples. Mailboxes rusted off their mounts, and sometimes people even forgot for a moment why they stopped by the post office for their mail rather than have it delivered. Over time, antifreeze purchases at the hardware store could be completed without comment, but Jesse Champee could never be spoken of without a pause for dour reflection, for thoughts of Petunia were never far away. On election night, 1992, as the patrons of the Sawdust watched the results come in, Stu Clutterbuck read aloud a letter he'd found among his fireplace kindling. No one looked grateful of this reminder, nor Stu's follow-up comment: "She wanted full run of that man. She's certainly tied her name to his, like it or not." He then ordered a Jagermeister with a Miller chaser.

Richard Weems is a retired teacher living in New York.

You can find more about Richard Weems at www.WeemsNet.net.